Also by Christine Regan Lake

My Body Cleanse

Circle of Healing For Women

www.ChristineReganLake.com

Sophia's Lovers

CHRISTINE REGAN LAKE

First Printing: 2014

ISBN 978-0-9903786-0-0 (sc)
ISBN 978-0-9903786-1-7 (e)

Christine Lake
Heartylicious, LLC
40590 North 50th Street
Cave Creek, AZ 85331

www.ChristineReganLake.com
Christine@heartylicious.com

Cover image: "Luna" copyright 2013
Original Oil Pastel by Christine Regan Lake

Ordering Information:
Special discounts are available on quantity purchases by corporations, associations, educators, and others. For details, contact the publisher at the above listed address.

U.S. trade bookstores and wholesalers: Please contact:
Christine at Christine@heartylicious.com

For you...

This book is dedicated to everyone who has
ever dreamed of having 'more' ...
in life and love.

May you find the courage to speak your truth, step into
your fear and love yourself enough to allow the greatest
blessings this world has to offer to enter your life.

May you find the life you crave and the love you deserve.

With warmth and love,

Christine

Dedication

This book is dedicated to my sons Parker and Cooper,
two beautiful, kind and intelligent young men in the making.
May you always have the courage to follow your dreams
wherever they may lead you, even if it scares you.
May you have the strength to take all the hardest blows that life
may send your way while remaining connected to the
softest and gentlest parts of yourselves.
May you always have belief in yourself and know
that you are loved and worthy of all your dreams.
May you have the wisdom to always make time
for what is most important.
May you always have a grateful heart
for the blessings that you have and continue to receive.
May you remain open to new adventures, possibilites and knowledge
that the universe will invariable send your way.
May you have the integrity to live your truth,
own your life and your mistakes
and not be afraid to admit when you are wrong.
May you decide to take the time to 'know thyself'
as it is one of the most incredible journeys that you will ever take.
May you find and experience the deepest and most beautiful love
that your heart can ever desire and remember to cherish it always.
May you learn to 'let go' of the need for control and trust
that your life is unfolding as it should when you are living your truth.
May you release whatever angers you may have for any injustices
you may have endured as it will only rob your life of precious energy.
May you laugh every single day of your life.
It is its own form of oxygen.
May you always know that my love for you is unconditional.
May you know that you don't have to earn it with praise
or accomplishments because it is always there for you,
like the sun and the moon and the stars.

Acknowledgements

"What is the recipe for successful achievement? To my mind there are just four essential ingredients: choose a career you love, give it the best there is in you, seize your opportunities, and be a member of a team."
                                                          - Benjamin Franklin Fairless

I would like to thank a number of special people who have contributed to my bringing "Sophia's Lovers" into fruition and supported my efforts in promoting this novella. It has been both a scary and exciting journey and I am grateful for all the support that I have received from this special group of people.

A very special thanks in no particular order;

Ellen Reach, Michael Lake, Theresa Radtke, Kevin Nelson, Carl Kinlan, Chris Szazz, Kristine Porter, Michael DePaul, Walter V. Tomasheski, Joseph Devine, Joanne Lombardi Synon, Marilyn Dale, Diane Massey, Anne Palmer, Laura Oppitz and to all my friends on facebook who encouraged me all through this process. You are awesome! Many, many thanks.

*S*ophia could feel the warmth of the sun shining down upon her face as she ran along the desolate and flower-filled backcountry road. She cherished running on Johnsontown Road for the woods were such a peaceful respite, open meadows with wildlife all around and the sounds of the fast flowing river running alongside it. Jogging for her was a meditation … feeling the weight of her body as her feet fell to the ground with each step. She devoured the sights and smells as the cool air lightly caressed her flushed cheeks. Her ears lovingly embraced the sounds of the rustling leaves on the trees and the occasional scamper of some animal amidst the bushes. She had always felt most at home in nature. It was her cathedral. It is where she prayed. It was where she could sort out her thoughts. As she was engulfing herself in the sounds of nature she heard her favorite dance song come on. "Oh" she smiled… She quickly dialed the sound up until it was almost deafening. She loved to immerse herself fully in the notes and allow her body to move effortlessly to the techno dance music. Her measured steps slowly morphed into a half dance/half run. Her hips swayed and her shoulders rolled to the rhythm and a massive smile exploded across her face… a joyful ecstasy began to flood her body as the music seeped into every crevice of her beautiful body.

His hands on the wheel were loose, the casual hold of autopilot. He took the curves of this road like he'd done for years, fast, very fast. Driving was his escape. There was nothing quite like being behind the wheel of his Bugatti Veyron to help him wipe his brain clean of all the muck from the day. The electric blue car was a sculpted masterpiece with the sexiest lines he had ever seen. With 16 powerful cylinders under the hood it was the speed that seduced him most about this car. He could hit 150 miles an hour in only 9 seconds. He had always been a speed freak from as early as he could remember. He'd had a number of serious accidents on several of his motorcycles throughout the years because of his addiction to speed. He'd been lucky, very lucky. After his last accident he sold his bikes and bought this Bugatti. It was an incredible sensation to have this extraordinary machine at your beck and call, to obey your every whim. It was the ultimate feeling of being in control with 4,160 lbs. of lusciousness at his fingertips. The car's sharp maneuverability at its top speed was insane. It was like a mind-altering hallucinatory trip as the adrenaline flooded your body when you were driving one. His mind played back the events of the day like a film... a dark noir film. As the film began unfolding the all too familiar feeling began to creep back into his stomach... a poisonous brew of anger, bile and regret. He could feel the tightness starting to creep into his limbs. His hands clenched down harder on the steering wheel and his foot took on a leaden weight as it pushed down harder on the gas pedal. The car's acceleration felt good, too good. It was as if the speed were setting him free. As if the faster he went, the faster he could get away from the torment and the dread that was inching through every cell of his body. In some small corner of his brain a red light started to flash... trying to warn him that he was going too fast and needed to slow down. The drug of escape, however, was far too great. It offered too much temporary solace to heed the warning. When the car locked-up on the gravel as it came around the bend, he lost control. The shiny blue bullet careened right into and over Sophia's delicate little frame. His eye's widened in shock at the horror of what just happened. His hands were clenched to the steering wheel as he tried to regain control. When the car finally stopped skidding and came to a stop he sat in stunned silence for a moment before looking in the rear view mirror at the poor woman in the road. He got out and ran back to Sophia. Her body lie contorted half on the road and half in the grass. There was blood splattered all over her white sweatshirt. Her well-worn sneaker was lying upside down just inches from her head. One of her ear buds had fallen out of her ear. He could hear the loud techno beats pulsing away. Blood was pooling out onto the pavement. He looked down at her and felt his stomach begin to heave. He felt his heart start to race and his breathing becoming faster. He blinked his eyes a few times as he started to see spots. He reached his arm down to the road for balance and took a few deep breaths. When he regained a bit of composure he turned back to Sophia and knelt down to see if he could help her. He heard the most grotesque gurgling sounds coming from her chest. Her lungs must have been filled with fluid, he thought. It was the most disturbing sound he'd ever heard. It was ugly. It was dark. It was the sound of death and it was his fault.

"I did this," he thought. His brain was trying to process all of this as he looked down into her face. She was looking up at him… the blood vessels in her eyes had burst and were filled with blood. It took all the courage he had … he looked directly into her eyes… silently, earnestly pleading with her to live… pleading for forgiveness. Her eyes communicated so much. He was amazed at what he saw. He saw no fear though. They were beautiful and soft and gentle. He could feel the penetration of her gaze… his heart started to fill with emotion… it was an overwhelming feeling. He didn't understand how he could feel this intense sense of peace enter him. It was cascading through out his entire being. He kept staring down into her eyes trying to figure out what was happening. Then, he understood.

He started to weep for this sweet fragile woman. He could see her lips starting to move; she was trying to say something. She whispered something, but he couldn't hear it. He moved his head down and put his ear directly next to her lips and she whispered, "Go."

He stared blankly down into her eyes not understanding. She whispered again, a bit more earnestly… "Go, now."

He stared back in silence. The gurgling sound in her chest got louder. His stomach started to churn and violently contract. It took all his focus to stay with her. He took her hand in his and he looked into her eyes as he pleaded with her.

"Please, please don't die, please don't die. I'm so sorry. I'm so, so sorry."

She looked at him and with what little energy she had left she smiled and shook her head ever so slightly and said… "They're here to take me home."

With that, he saw the most incredible white light shining down from the heavens. It completely enveloped both of them. He could feel heat from the light shining down on him as the most indescribable feeling started surging through his body. His heart began to fill even more as the tears were streaming down his face. In the next moment, he could feel the heat start to wane and the light slowly fade and then it was gone. When he looked back down into Sophia's eyes, they were frozen. She was gone.

He sat bent over her body, utterly immobile, trying to absorb what had just happened. He kept hearing her words over and over again… "Go"… "Go now"…

He stared down into her eyes as heaviness overtook his chest and a thick black film of death crept its way into every pocket of air in his lungs. He bit down hard on his lower lip. Tears streaked down his trembling face. A flash of pink caught his eye.

Sophia had a bright pink nylon rope bracelet on her wrist. He looked down at it for a few seconds before he bent down and took it off her wrist. He placed it in the palm of his hand and then folded his fingers around it. He closed his hands around it as if it were a sacred talisman, and the act a silent reverence. He needed something of hers… he didn't know why… he just knew that he was going to need her in the coming months. Something deep inside told him that he would need her strength and, her forgiveness.

He got up solemnly and walked back to his car and got inside. He sat slumped over the steering wheel weeping. Her blood splattered face in his head and the gurgling sounds of death thundering in his ears. He looked down at his hands. They were blood red and sticky. The sight of them made him dizzy. His stomach wrenched and he threw up all over the passenger seat. He was sobbing uncontrollably. He had lost track of any sense of time since the accident had happened. He was in some nightmare time warp and he couldn't escape. Time stood still in the face of death. He managed to take a few deep breaths, which helped to calm him down.

"You have to go, just like she said," he choked out through his sobs. He wiped his eyes, turned the key in the ignition, looked in the rear view mirror and slowly turned the car around. He stopped as he was passing her body and rolled down the window. He said a prayer in his head as he looked down at her limp, lifeless body. His stomach started to violently dry heave again. He wiped the tears from his eyes and whispered "I'm so sorry," and then slowly pulled the car away.

"Antonio"

ntonio was asleep when the sound of the phone startled him awake. He looked at the bedside clock, slowly his mind comprehended the numbers… 4:00 am… Who's calling at 4am? he thought, as he grabbed the cordless phone and sat himself up on the side of the bed. "Antonio," a woman whispered. His mind immediately registered the frail voice on the other end of the line; it was Claudia, Sophia's sister. His body went rigid. A thick, hard knot forming in the base of his throat as he spoke "Claudia, what's happened?"

"Antonio, she's gone. She's gone." Claudia exploded into tears.

"What do you mean she's gone, Claudia? Gone where? What are you talking about?"

"She's dead, Antonio, she's dead. She was hit by a car and left for dead. It was a hit and run."

There was silence. The words hit Antonio like a baseball bat slamming into his chest. He couldn't breathe. Tears welled up in his eyes and he tried to speak, but nothing would come out. There was nothing but dead air on the phone.

"Antonio… Antonio are you there?"…

He took a deep breath and cleared his throat…

"Yes… I'm here. How, Claudia? How did it happen?… Where is she now? I need to see her." Antonio was rambling.

"She was running on Johnsontown Road. I still can't believe it, Antonio. I can't believe she is dead."

"I'm coming over. Where are you?"…

"We're all at St. Vincent's." Claudia broke down sobbing… "She never even made it to the hospital," they said she died at the scene. She died all alone. She died on the side of the road alone. Can you imagine how terrifying that must have been for her? I just … I just don't know how I can bear this. She was my life … she was everything to me. I have to go. I'll see you when you get here." Claudia hung up.

Antonio held the phone tightly in his hand for several minutes before he reached over and hung it up. He closed his eyes as he sat perched on the edge of the bed. His mind started drifting from one memory to the next…

Sophia was sprawled out regally on a sun bleached wooden recliner. Every muscle in her beautifully sculpted body was completely relaxed. Elegantly draped on the chaise she looked like a Goddess painted on the wall of a sacred temple. Her physique was lean and sexy with one arm stretched above her head and one knee raised. The folds of her soft, flowing, crème-colored chiffon dress hung off the sides of the lounger. A smile that belied a deep peace spread across her perfect porcelain face as her jet black hair cascaded down the back of the chair. Her deep green emerald eyes lost in the clouds above. She was soaking in the perfection of this moment. She had dreamed of coming to Cinque Terre for as long as she could remember and now she was here, with Antonio.

The family-owned villa had a breathtaking view of the ocean and an expansive view of all the other buildings clinging to the side of the mountain in this centuries old village. The warm orangey-yellow paint on the building was flaking off and it reminded her of the painting that she had seen so many years ago that first planted this dreamy place in her heart. She could smell the wild flowers and the scent of the salt air from crashing waves below. She could hear a passing street vendor yelling a warm 'hello' to one of the shopkeepers. She was letting all of this sensorial sweetness seep deep inside her when Antonio stormed out onto the veranda. His face was taut with anger and flush red. As he started his tirade, a vein began to pulse at the side of his forehead. It was very unbecoming. Sophia could feel her body begin to tense up—his poisonous, negative energy assaulting her senses.

"I can't believe this. I can't fucking believe his audacity. I'm furious," Antonio ranted as his hand went flying into the air. "John is trying to screw me over. I knew it. I should have known better than to get involved with him. What the hell was I thinking? I'm killing myself at that restaurant and I finally take a vacation and he sends me this fucking email with a list of problems and then says he needs to take a loan from the business. Who the hell does he think he is? And, what does he think …I'm a bank? I'm just supposed to bankroll him. This is bullshit, total bullshit. I'm so disgusted right now. I'm really at the end of my rope with him. I think I'm going to have to part ways with him on this restaurant and just buy him out. I can't deal with this kind of shit all the time."

Sophia, jolted out of her blissful euphoria, simply stared at Antonio in disbelief as he raged on ranting for another few minutes until he was finally out of breath.

He stopped, looked at Sophia and venomously shouted… "Aren't you going to say anything? Don't you even care? I'm completely exhausted from killing myself at work and my partner is trying to screw me over… Don't you care? Don't you have anything to say?"

Sophia got up from the chaise slowly without saying a word. She came and stood in front of Antonio. She took a deep breath, looked directly into his deeply wounded eyes and then slapped him across the face. The sound of the slap seemed to echo, holding on into the ocean air. Her hand was red from the impact and his cheek burned. Antonio's eyes shot wide open. He rubbed his cheek with his hand and shot her a cold, confused look…

"What the hell was that for?"…

"Do I have anything to say?… Yes, I have something to say. I'm not your mother, Antonio. I'm not here to coddle you. I'm not here to lull you back to sleep. I'm your lover. I'm here to wake you up. Wake you up to everything that life has to offer. Let me tell you something—you are exhausted because you are running as hard and as fast as you can every day from that relentless and incessant voice in your head that keeps telling you that you are not enough, that you are not worthy. That voice that keeps telling you that you have to prove yourself. You can't run forever Antonio… at some point you have to face yourself. You have to face your wounds. I have tried in as many ways as I can possibly think of to show you and to tell you what a magnificent man you are. That you are perfect just the way you are…but you won't listen. You won't hear me. You won't let me in. You are missing out on life and you don't even see it. You are so caught up in the past that you are missing your life.

Had you been here... now... you would have felt the perfection of this moment... the smell of the salty sea air in your nose, the sounds of the waves. You would have felt the love in my heart that I feel for you. If you were HERE... you would have walked in and felt that flood of love enter your heart and you would have taken me in your arms and made love to me right on this veranda. Instead, you storm out here with your anger and your indignation and you shit all over it. If you want to throw your life away going to battle with your demons every day, that's your choice... but my life is sacred... every moment of it... and you have no right to steal it from me."

The sadness began to well up and spill over from her eyes. Her throat went dry and her voice was barely audible.

"I love you with every ounce of my being, Antonio... but I'm running out of words. I'm running out of air"... she turned and walked inside the villa.

Antonio stared after her for some time. He looked down at his cell phone and then slid it into his side pocket. He moved his eyes to where Sophia had been sitting. He saw a bottle of Veuve Cliquot Pink Champagne. Her favorite, he thought. The bottle stood next to two beautiful crystal glasses and a small exquisitely designed black velvet box sitting on the table. He walked over and picked it up. It was heavy. He closed his eyes. A painful sigh slipped from his lips.

He untied the red velvet bow and opened the box. It was a gold Breguet pocket watch. He found his entire body was tensing up and his breathing was getting shallow. He opened the watch. Inscribed inside in an elegant script, it said simply. 'Time for love and kisses—Sophia.' He felt a stab of pain in his chest. He sat down in the chair and began to massage the pain with his hand.

"Martin"

As Martin Forsythe opened up the morning paper he could smell the Hacienda Las Esmeralda brewing across the room. With its thick texture, deep flavor and that incredible aroma, it was his favorite way to start the day. Browsing the paper, as he usually did each morning, always on the hunt for that next script idea, his eyes abruptly stopped at the photo of Sophia and the corresponding headline about the hit and run.

He stared down at the photo. His eyes locked on hers. He could feel an odd mixture of emotions building in his chest... something warm and soft, yet swirling within that was an anxiousness ... that quirky feeling he always got in his gut when he knew he was on to something. He didn't know how long he remained fixed on her photo. He had become lost in her eyes. Martin was a man who lived his life from his gut. Every decision he had ever made came straight from his gut. It was an instantaneous knowing and it was screaming loudly at the moment, just like always. "Who is this woman?" he continued to mutter to himself... Her eyes penetrating like a laser beam, fierce and raw. They have a pureness to them, strong, yet etched with vulnerability.

He had looked into enough eyes during thousands of auditions throughout his 30 plus year career as a film director to notice immediately when there was something special about a woman. The eyes reveal all, one's soul reflecting back at you, a true looking glass into the deepest part of one's humanity. He devoured the story quickly and then read it again and then once again. He went to the drawer and pulled out a pen and paper and wrote down the information for her wake and funeral service and then picked up his coffee mug and walked into his study to gather himself in his favorite brown leather chair. Worn from years of use, this chair had been with him since his first days in Hollywood. It was a sacred spot. It was warm and safe. It was home. He started each day sitting in this chair and thinking about what he wanted to accomplish for the day and taking a moment to be thankful for everything that he felt grateful for. This was his version of meditating. As he sat drinking his beloved Panamanian coffee, his eyes wandered around the room. He scanned the shelves that were packed with hundreds of scripts and journals. He worked his way over to his glass curio cabinet filled with cinematic awards of every category. My life's work, he thought.

He'd absolutely loved every moment of his exceptional career. He'd been very blessed and he knew it. He seemed to have a gift and yet, recently, he had noticed that he felt restless. A stirring inside to go someplace that he had never gone creatively. A relentless yearning that would not let go of him, to reach deeper within himself. A desire... NO... a NEED... to say something important, something that would matter. He'd made millions of dollars on comic relief and action adventure films, but they felt dead to him right now. There was a new chapter opening up to him and he needed to follow it. He needed to stumble into the darkness, even though it scared him. His brain started in on its familiar routine. Why would you veer from a proven formula for success? This new idea was risky. He knew that. He had seen directors before him step outside their safety zone and fail miserably. Fail publicly.

It's one thing to have a personal failure of yours that was known only to you—to not meet some silent, personal goal. It is quite another thing to fail miserably in front of all your colleagues, in front of the world. The failure of a movie is a very public thing. Everyone knows it and then you find your name in a different category. You are no longer a safe bet with the money people. Now you are a risk and the money people don't like risks. They like proven formulas. It helps them sleep better at night.

He had never gone down this kind of road before. "Ludicrous"... slipped out of his mouth like a swear, but he couldn't stop thinking about it. He knew he had to follow this feeling... even though he didn't understand why. His stomach began to tighten as he thought of Sophia's funeral and where it might lead.

He closed his eyes and took a few deep breaths and then started to repeat the little mantra his secretary Marilyn had taught him… "Inhale with certainty and exhale the doubt." Within a few moments the churning in his stomach dissipated. He opened his eyes. He felt clear again. What a handy little thing. He laughed to himself and then placed his mug down on the table next to the article. He took one last look at her eyes and then rose to head for the shower.

"Finn"

There was black ice on the streets and a biting Siberian wind was blowing through the small town. The rain and hail was blowing sideways and pelting the side of the car. The sound of the ice chunks hammering into his door unnerved Finn who was waiting for the light to turn green. The car behind him honked his horn obnoxiously. Finn looked up to see that the light had turned green. He looked in the rearview mirror and grumbled "asshole."

He shook his head, blinked his eyes a few times, looked both ways and then slowly made the right turn onto Wilson Avenue. Cars were jammed in every possible space all the way down the street leading up to Dohaney's Funeral Home. He recognized several people as they were scurrying under their umbrellas to make it to the building without getting drenched. He drove past the funeral home hoping to find a parking spot further down the street. He continued down the narrow road, simply to find that there were just as many cars down at this end of the road as well. "What a nightmare," he whispered as his eyes scanned the sides of the road. He finally reached the end of the cars, pulled in front of a black Range Rover and parked. He turned off the ignition, undid his seatbelt and placed the keys in his suit jacket. He sat back in the seat and let his head fully relax against the headrest. He closed his eyes and took a long deep breath. He sat there for a few moments trying to gather his composure to go inside.

As he closed his eyes he could see Sophia's face. He remembered the last time that he had kissed her. He remembered the feel of her lips, the taste of her mouth and the scent of perfume on her neck. His heart wrenched. He pushed her image out of his head and took another deep breath. He sat forward and reached for the door handle and began to open the door. As his arm swung the door open, the torrential rains flooded down and soaked his suit jacket. "Goddamn it," he screamed and quickly slammed the door shut. Finnegan could feel the anger inside him welling up. "Goddamn it," he screamed again and punched the center of the steering wheel as he burst into tears for the first time since hearing the news of Sophia's death. He grabbed the steering wheel tightly and squeezed it as hard as he could trying to force out all the horrible pain in his chest that was consuming him. His cell phone rang but he let it go to voicemail. Time passed as he sat there. Eventually he could hear voices. It was the couple coming back to the Range Rover parked behind him. Their voices were muffled; he couldn't make out what they were saying.

He looked at his watch, 8:30pm, only thirty more minutes left in the showing, he thought. He looked in the rearview mirror to catch a glimpse of himself. He looked rough. He rubbed his bloodshot eyes. He buttoned the top button of his shirt and repositioned his tie. He reached over and grabbed his bottle of Evian and took a few sips and then pulled out his cell phone to see who had called. It was his mother. He hit play and then put the phone up to his ear to playback the message.

"Finn, honey, it's me. I'm here at the funeral home and I was wondering if everything is ok? Are you doing all right? I thought you were coming. I love you so much. I'm here for you." He could hear the tears as she spoke softly. She had always loved Sophia dearly and had hoped that they would have married. Sophia was the daughter she'd never had.

Finnegan closed his phone and slid it into his pants pocket. He reached over and grabbed the umbrella off the floor before opening the door. The rain had since died down and was now not more than a freezing drizzle. He walked toward the funeral home at a strong pace. He wanted to have time to talk to Claudia. He felt bad that he was getting there so late.

As he approached the building he could see the line was still out the door. It was no surprise; so many people loved Sophia. She had so many friends from all the different areas of her life. He heard the rain hitting the water in the pond as he made his way across the small bridge that led to the funeral home. He positioned himself at the back of the line and waited his turn.

The line moved slowly, there were many people. He'd always hated funerals. What the hell do you say? He'd always thought… but now… this was unthinkable. This wasn't just some elder family member who'd reached the end of a long and healthy life that had been well lived. This was SOPHIA. He rubbed his chest, as a sharp, stabbing pain seemed to pierce it.

A few more couples came up behind him and took their place in line. Inch by inch he made his way up the line and closer to the building. It took about twenty minutes for him to finally make it inside. He picked up the pen to sign the book. The pen held in mid air just a few inches from the book. What the hell do I write? He looked down at the book and read a few of the last few entries. He felt a twinge in his chest sending a shot of pain in a circular motion out from his heart. He knew he had to write something.

"Sophia will never truly be gone because she lives on in those who knew her. Her love and kindness are timeless and can still be felt by all those whose lives she touched. Sophia will be with us always.—Finnegan O'Sullivan" He put the pen down and turned to head into the viewing room.

It was Claudia who saw him first. She came right over and gave Finn a long, hard squeeze. They stood there hugging in silence for a few minutes. Both of them knew there was nothing you could say, that sometimes a hug said a thousand things that words could not. When they finally pulled apart, both of them were weeping. Finn spoke first. "How are you doing Claudia? I'm so sorry I haven't called. I couldn't. I've been in shock, to be honest. I just… I mean… I just still can't believe it. It just seems so surreal."

Claudia shook her head in agreement. "I know, Finny, I know." Claudia didn't even try to put on a strong face. She didn't need to with Finn. Of all the men that Sophia had ever loved, Finn was Claudia's favorite. Finn and she had a strong connection, almost like siblings. They both loved Sophia so much.

"Honestly, Finny… I'm a fucking wreck. I feel like the life has been sucked right out of me. I really don't know how you go on after something like this. Most days I'm just barely breathing, you know what I mean? I'm trying to hold it together for Mom's sake because she is taking it worse than I am."

"Yeah, I can imagine. It must be gut-wrenching for her." He took her hand and squeezed it. "But you are a strong woman and I know you will figure out how to make it through and I know your Mom will too. She is one tough lady and she's been through a lot. You guys just have to be there for each other. Have you heard from the police? Do they have any suspects, yet?"

Claudia started to cry again as she shook her head. Finn reached around her again and gave her a tight squeeze. "Is there anything you need? Anything I can I help you with?" She pulled a ragged tissue from her black suit jacket and wiped her nose. "I, uh… I don't know… I have to go through her stuff in her apartment. I don't know if I'm up for doing it by myself. Do you think you might be able to help me go through it?"

"Of course, you let me know when and I'll be there. And, for anything else you and your Mom need. Okay?—Please don't hesitate to call me. I mean it."

"Thanks so much, Finn." She hugged him again. "I'd better let you go so you can say hello to Mom. She's been looking for you. She wants to see you."… "Okay, I'll go right over to her now." "I love you, Finny, so good to see you. I've missed you."

"I've missed you, too, sweetie."

Finnegan made his way through the crowd and over to Sophia's Mom. She saw him just as he was about to say hello.

"Finny… oh, Finny. I'm so glad you could make it. She stepped forward and embraced Finn with one of her soft, gentle hugs. She rubbed his back lightly as she whispered… "Thank you so much for coming, Finn. I was hoping you'd be able to make it." "Gianna, of course I would make it. Did you honestly think I might not come?"

"I don't know what I thought. I just wanted to see you, Finn." The tears were streaking down Gianna's cheeks. He could see the anguish etched in her face. She looked so fragile.

"Did you see all the photos we put together? There are some beautiful ones of you two. I tried to pick the one's I knew she really loved of the two of you."

"I didn't get a chance to look yet, I'll do that next. I wanted to come right over and talk to you first."

"You are so sweet, Finny. Thank you for that."

"Nothing to thank me for, it's the truth."

"I saw your mother before. I'm not sure where she is right now, but she was worried that you weren't here."

"Yeah, she left me a message on my cell phone." Finn looked into Gianna's eyes. "She loved Sophia very much."

She looked back at Finn "I know she did. Sophia always felt that."

A tall gentleman came up and placed his hand on Gianna's arm and she turned and looked at him. She smiled and he reached in and gave her a hug. Finn watched for a moment and then turned and walked away.

"Final Words"

It was one of those picturesque mornings that you see in the opening scene of your favorite feel good movie. The sun was blindingly bright; the sweet fragrant smell of hibiscus wafting through the air and the temperature was a perfect 82 degrees. It was one of those mornings that seems to seep into the marrow of your being with the belief that everything is going to be fine… it seemed a fitting kind of feel for the day that was set aside to memorialize Sophia's life. It was as if God himself was saying… "Sophia's energy will shine through today for all to enjoy as her friends and family come to celebrate her life."

Tristan was sitting in the back room of the funeral home going over his notes. He felt deeply honored that Sophia's family asked him to deliver the eulogy. He'd spent the last three days trying to encapsulate Sophia's life… who she was and what she stood for. It was one of the most difficult tasks he had ever done. How to summarize a person's life? How does one summarize someone as extraordinary as Sophia?

It was a question that bore a lot of weight in the answering. It felt like a Herculean task for which he was not prepared, but he could not let Sophia's family down. He felt an incredible responsibility to them, and to Sophia.

He sat nervously waiting to be called to give the eulogy as he contemplated what his life would have been like had he never met Sophia. Without a doubt, she had had a tremendous influence on his life. The five years he spent with her were the most transformational years of his adult life. Before he met Sophia, he was dead, and didn't even know it. His life was full of things and activities… but it was a life that was STERILE.

His fingers were running up and down the sides of the folded loose-leaf paper. He had practiced reading the eulogy so many times the paper was a wrinkled mess. He had a sick feeling in his stomach. He was scared that he was not going to be able to make it through his speech without breaking down into tears. He had written and re-written this eulogy so many times trying to boil it down to the essentials—trying to capture the most important parts of who Sophia was and what she stood for. He hoped he had been able to capture it.

He heard the funeral director gathering everyone into the room and then introduced him. He stood up, ran his fingers through his hair, looked down at his paper, adjusted his jacket and then closed his eyes and said softly to himself, as if it were a prayer... I love you, Sophia. I hope I do you proud. His eyes filled with tears. He took a deep breath and walked into the room. He could feel his chest tighten and his stomach harden. He took his position at the podium and looked out into the crowd. There had to be 200 people jammed into the little room and pouring out into the hallway. He looked out into the audience moving from face to face. He paused for another moment, took a long, silent breath and looked down at his speech that he'd placed on the stand. He looked back up at the crowded room and all the eyes staring at him and then crumpled up the piece of paper.

"Good morning, ladies and gentleman. My name is Tristan Maddox. First, let me say, thank you for joining us today in celebrating the life of Sophia Antonetti. As I am sure you know, she was an extraordinary lady. Those of you in this room should consider yourself lucky that you were blessed to have had her in your life. I wanted to share with you today some thoughts about the woman who was the brightest light that I have ever met."

He paused for a moment, looked around the room and then began again.

"I had a carefully crafted eulogy that I wrote for all of you today, but as I looked down at it, I realized that that is not what Sophia would have wanted. You see, in a certain sense, she didn't believe in 'carefully crafted'... She believed in living your life in the moment and to embrace the 'messiness of life'... to be fully present and know that EVERYTHING you think or feel in that moment is real, right and authentic and deserved to be honored... She taught me that every emotion that you feel is SACRED... "I realized, as I stepped up to the podium, if I read you some perfectly crafted piece of writing... it would be an insult to her. So, instead, I am going to do this straight from my heart and just be with you and share whatever it is that comes to my heart and mind as I am here with you right now. THAT, I believe, is the kind of eulogy that she deserves and would have wanted."

You could hear the outlet of carefully stifled tears being released and the sounds of people blowing their noses. The room was teaming with pain and sorrow.

"I can see by the looks on your faces and all the tears and sobs I hear, that you are as heartbroken as I am to have lost Sophia. I don't claim to understand why something like this had to happen. I don't understand the bigger picture. All I can do is cherish the gifts that I received from her, while we were together, and endeavor to share those truths that she taught me, with others. If I ask myself what gifts did she give me, I find that there were so many it is hard to say... so I guess the more important question is... What were the most profound gifts she gave me? What were the most life changing things that she taught me?

"Before I met Sophia, I had a great life. I was very successful in my business and I had a large circle of friends and I had the luxury of traveling around the world, but honestly, my life was superficial. There was no depth to it. I was not someone who took the time to look in the mirror and ask myself Who am I? Why am I here?... I didn't see the value in those questions then. I didn't recognize what I was missing out on by not asking myself those questions, by not taking the time to travel to the deepest parts of myself to discover what I believed and what I wanted my life to stand for."

I had no idea when I met her how different my life would be. When you are in an intimate relationship with someone like Sophia, it can't help but change you. When you are with someone who so completely cherished their life and took nothing for granted, someone who every single day of their life woke up and said, "How can I be better today? How can I be kinder? ... More compassionate? ... More understanding?" it was inspiring.

"She was someone who continually challenged herself to be more and to give more. She was someone who knew deeply and with total clarity who she was and why she was put on this earth. When you are with someone like that, it cannot help but rub off on you. It cannot help but make you pause and look at yourself in the mirror and begin to ask yourself the same questions."

"The man I am today is a very different man than the one who first met Sophia that rainy day in the subway. Her passion for truth and her spiritual evolution as a human being was the most inspiring thing I have ever witnessed, and been blessed to experience firsthand. She taught me how to take complete responsibility for my own life. She blamed no one for anything in her life and took total ownership for everything she said or did, every single day. And, beyond that, she fully owned it when she might slip up and have a bad moment. She would immediately take steps to fix anything she might have unknowingly done to hurt someone's feelings."

"When I met Sophia I was an atheist, I believed in nothing and I was very disconnected from humanity. Please don't get me wrong, I gave money to charities because I thought that is what you do when you are fortunate, but I felt no personal visceral connection to anyone who wasn't in my intimate circle. Sophia used to always say that we were all connected. When I first met her I thought she meant that in a 'love thy neighbor' kind of way, instead of the literal sense in which she meant it. She meant the literal energetic connection that we have with each other."

"I had never experienced, nor even really known, what she meant when she talked about having a 'soul-to-soul connection' with someone when she did her Reiki sessions… when she could connect her life force with another human being. It was astonishing to me. Sophia not only gave me the gift of discovering who I was, but she gave my body back to me. She taught me how to INHABIT my body, to understand the LANGUAGE of the BODY."

The room was silent. Tristan looked out into the audience and caught eyes with Gianna. All of the love that Tristan had ever felt for Sophia poured out of his eyes and into her. You could see her absorbing it. You could see the energy flowing into her by the look on her face. She closed her eyes and inhaled deeply. There was no one else in the room at that moment except she and Tristan… just the two of them bathed in the love they both felt for Sophia.

After a few moments Gianna opened her eyes. She looked at Tristan and then she lifted her hand to her mouth and she blew him a kiss. Through a blur of tears Tristan smiled and shook his head as if to say, … I know.

Tristan raised his gaze back to the attendees. "At this time, I would like to ask everyone to stand up and please clasp hands. I would like to play one of Sophia's favorite songs "Now We Are Free," and pay tribute to one of the most beautiful woman who ever lived. This is for Sophia."

The music came on and the soothing song started to swell within the room. The sumptuous sounds of the instruments slowly starting to mute out the sounds of sobbing. Claudia clasped Finn's hand tightly, her eyes squeezed shut as tears streamed down her cheeks. Finn's eyes were closed as he held Sophia's vision in his head. Tristan stood next to Gianna, his thumb stroking the top of her palm and then he leaned over and kissed the top of her head. Antonio was in the very back of the room. He didn't know the woman whose hand he held. It shook in his hand while he held it. She was weeping. He squeezed it, comfortingly.

He felt a dead weight in his chest. It was hard for him to breathe. If there had been anyone who had not yet cried, this song would have wrung it out of them. The beauty, power and emotion of it was intense. Which is why Sophia had loved it so much, thought Antonio nostalgically. Tears were flowing heavily as the beautiful song came to a close. The funeral director came in and announced that they would be forming up the caravan to head to the gravesite for whomever wanted to join them.

Claudia slowly made her way to the back room to get her jacket. When she opened the door she was startled to see someone sitting across the room in the corner. As she moved further into the dark, quiet room she saw that it was Leonardo. He looked up when he heard her come in. His face was carved with anguish. He had dark circles under his eyes and his long, angular face looked leaden, dark and weary. He simply looked at her. He said nothing. What was there to say, they both thought simultaneously.

She walked over and sat down next to him on the stiff, formal couch and slid her hand into his and closed it tightly into hers. They sat there in silence for several minutes before he spoke.

"I'm sorry I didn't come in Claudia. I just couldn't. I couldn't bring myself to walk in and see her like that."

"I know Leo, honey. I know. If you don't think you can, then maybe you shouldn't, maybe you should just remember her as she was."

Leo squeezed her hand gently in reply. They could hear the crowd of people outside the door mulling about. Leonardo broke the silence.

"How is your Mom doing?"…

"She's breathing, like all of us. That's about all that we can manage at the moment." Claudia started to cry again, a full unrestrained bawling.

Leo wrapped his long, lean arms around her to comfort her. He gave her a strong, loving embrace to squeeze out all the hurt and pain. He held her for a few moments and then began his own release… his own confession.

"There were things I should have said to her, Claudia, things I wanted to say, but never did. She deserved better than that. She deserved to know how I felt." "Leo, she knew you loved her. She knew. I promise you that. Please, don't ever doubt that. She loved you deeply. She cherished her time with you. You must know how special you were to her, don't you?"

Leonardo closed his eyes and tears ran down his face. "Thank you, Claudia, thank you so much for saying that. Sometimes I believe it, and sometimes I don't."

Someone knocked on the door and then it opened, it was the funeral director. "Claudia, I think your mother is looking for you. I think she needs you. She's looking a little overwhelmed."

Claudia looked up. "Of course, I'm coming."

She turned back to Leonardo and conjured up her best strong face and smiled. "Got to go, Mom needs me. They are forming up the procession. Are you coming?"…

He looked at her for a moment, "Yes, I'm coming. I'll be there."… "Okay, we better head out then."

"I'm just going to take a few moments to say goodbye to Sophia first."…

They stood up and Claudia gave Leonardo a long, strong hug and then kissed him on the cheek.

"Love you, Leo... we'll get through this." He kissed her back on the forehead and he whispered... "Yeah."

Claudia turned around and walked out of the room and Leo headed to the Memorial room to say goodbye to Sophia. There was no one left in the room when Leonardo entered. The room was like a garden. There were beautiful colored flowers everywhere: roses, tulips, carnations, orchids and exotic ones he couldn't even name. He stopped to look at the collage that someone had made with dozens of photos of her. There were pictures of her from every stage of her life. There were photos of her and her Mom and Dad, she and Claudia as kids.

His eyes were roaming the board when he stopped at a picture of he and Sophia at a friend's wedding. He looked at the photo and remembered it vividly. It had been an incredible night. He remembered sitting in the service thinking about his wedding to Sophia... what it would be like, to be married to her.

He had no idea that day that that dream would not come true. He noticed a sudden pang in his chest. He lifted his hand to the spot and started rubbing it. Without a sound, he walked up to the casket and knelt down before it. It took him a few moments before he could bring himself to look at her. He started to sob heavily. His chest was heaving. "I'm so sorry, Sophia. I'm sorry I wasn't the man you needed me to be. I'm sorry I couldn't give you what you needed."

He reached into his pocket and pulled out an envelope with her name on it. He held the envelope in his hands... "I don't know if wherever you are you will be able to know what is in this... to finally know what is and was always in my heart. I'm sorry it took me losing you to realize how much you meant to me. I wish I could have been able to tell you these things when we were together. You deserved to know it. You deserved to hear it from me. Please forgive me, Sophia," he whispered. He placed the envelope in the casket next to her and he leaned down and kissed the top of her forehead. He looked at her for one last moment and then slowly stood up and headed out of the room to join the procession.

As he walked out of the funeral home he saw cars lined up down the street. He walked over to his black Mercedes, climbed inside and then made his way to the back of the processional. He turned the CD player on and listened to "Now We Are Free" once again. He'd been listening to it ever since he had heard about Sophia's death.

He watched as friends and family members hugged and consoled each other. He saw the pain and heartache on their faces. There was nothing like the death of someone you love to make you stop and take stock of everything in your life. He'd certainly been doing that. He knew that Sophia's death was a wake up call for him. He knew that there was no way he was going to let her death go without meaning… he was going to use this moment as an opportunity to grow and to heal.

As those thoughts resonated within him, a sense of peace washed through him for the first time since this nightmare began.

"Antonio's Reflections"

ntonio had made his way out of the service quickly. He didn't feel like talking with anyone right now. He was sitting in his car waiting and watching as the people came out of the funeral home. His car was directly behind the limo. He was here for Sophia, Claudia and her Mother, that was it. He didn't want to engage with anyone about Sophia. He didn't have the strength for it. He'd been living in a fog since Claudia had called him with the news. He had been utterly distracted and unable to focus on anything. The grief, the heaviness, the darkness that was overtaking him was intense. He was not very good about handling his emotions. He felt angry. He felt gypped. He had raged on at God for days trying to understand.

His hands tightened on the steering wheel. He caught himself and had to laugh, the laughter was an exhale, a release. After all the time I spent with her and all she taught me, I still can't allow myself to accept what is.

He closed his eyes and inhaled as deeply as he could. His chest was constricted in anguish. He reached down into his pocket and pulled out the gold pocket watch Sophia had given him. He squeezed his hand tightly around it and slowly closed his eyes…

Antonio sat in the recliner on the veranda listening to the waves crash beneath him. A wave of shame rolled through him as he thought about his actions. He realized what a self-absorbed asshole he had been when he stormed out and yelled at Sophia. He could feel a heaviness overtaking him. He lowered his head. She didn't deserve that. She had arranged this incredible moment for us, gone to so much effort to make this moment in Cinque Terre something beautiful, that they would never forget, and he fucked it up. His temper had ruined it. It was not the first time.

He shook his head in disgust. It was a shitty pattern he seemed to keep repeating. He slipped the pocket watch into his pocket and then looked over at the Champagne. He reached over, opened it and poured two glasses. He picked up the glasses, got up and walked inside, not having the vaguest idea what he was going to say to her, but knowing that he needed to apologize. He walked into the villa and went from room to room until he found her in the bathroom. She was soaking in a bubble bath. The room was a cloud of pure steam and water was fogged up on the mirror. Her eyes were covered with a warm, wet washcloth and her arms rested on the sides of the tub. Her skin was wet with perspiration.

With one knuckle he knocked on the door... "Can I come in?"... There was silence... "Sophia, honey... please... can I come in."... It took her a moment to answer.

Her voice was stiff and you could tell she had been crying... "What do you want, Antonio?"...

He looked in tenuously. "I don't even know what I want to say. Sorry seems so pathetic a word for how badly I feel. You didn't deserve that. I had no right to do that to you. I don't know what happens to me when I get like that. I don't mean to take it out on you. I just get so furious and then I explode."

He paused for a moment and then continued.

"I know I need to make some serious changes. I'm ashamed of my behavior. I'm ashamed that I yelled at you like that. I feel awful that I ruined this night. That was such a beautiful thing you did."

He looked down at her under the mound of bubbles and then continued. "I love the pocket watch, but I feel like every time I look at it, I will be reminded of what an asshole I am. How can I make this up to you, Sophia? How can I show you how much I love you?"

The room was quiet except for the fizzling pop of the soap bubbles dissipating.... Antonio waited ... it felt like minutes had passed.... Finally, she responded...

"I just don't want this relationship to be so hard, Antonio... Love shouldn't have to be this difficult, this painful. I love you and I know that you have issues, we all do, but when you don't heal your wounds… they come back and get lashed out on me. You have this stockpile of anger that you have never dealt with towards your father and it leaks out all over me. That's how anger works, Antonio… unless you face it and heal it… you just keep recycling it and hurling it at those closest to you." She shook her head back and forth in dismay.

"I haven't betrayed you, Antonio. I didn't do anything to deserve your hurling that crap at me. This isn't the first time you've done it either."

"I know," he whispered, as he nodded his head.

"How can I trust that you aren't going to keep doing this?"

"I guess I have to rebuild that trust. I know that words are cheap and the only way that I can show you that I want to change is by my actions. I'm asking you Sophia… where do I start? … Where do I begin to start unraveling this stuff?"…

"I can give you some ideas, just not now… I'm exhausted. I'm not up for diving into all that right now. I just want to relax and enjoy the warm water and try and forget about what just happened."

"Of course. I brought you a glass of Champagne. Would you like it?"

She lifted the washcloth off of her eyes and looked over at him. She sighed a smile. "Sure."

He walked over and sat on the edge of the tub and handed her the glass. She took the glass and raised it to her lips and took a sip.

"Mmmmmmm…. I do love this"… she smiled as she enjoyed the bubbling sensation in her mouth.

Antonio reached over and placed his hand on her wet knee, wiped away some of the bubbles and then bent down and planted a slow, wet kiss on her lower thigh and then raised his head to look into her eyes. She looked into his eyes, they were begging for both forgiveness and permission. The sensual upturn of her mouth gave him what he had been seeking.

She brought the champagne glass to her mouth and took another sip as he put his head back down and kissed her inner thigh again and again as he made his way higher and higher. A soft moan escaped her lips as she felt his lips upon her skin. She closed her eyes as she squeezed both of her legs closed around Antonio's body. He reached down with his other hand and put his glass down on the floor and then proceeded to run both of his hands down the insides of her thigh as he moved his way closer and closer to her spot. The sleeves of his shirt were soft and tickly as they rubbed against her wet, waiting skin. With one movement Antonio was in the tub with her and pulled her into his arms. Her hungry body ached.

He ran his fingers through her hair and jerked her head back as he pulled her face into his and then turned it abruptly and moved her hair so he could devour her neck. He loved to tease her. She was defenseless when it came to her neck… it was like sliding a key into a treasure chest of pleasure.

As his tongue tantalized her skin, she grabbed a chunk of his hair and pulled it passionately. Her nipples hardened as her body ached to feel him inside of her. He pulled her face back around and sensuously kissed the sides of her mouth. She whispered, "stick out your tongue."

He responded immediately and with the slightest and softest motion she swept the edges of his tongue with her lips and then engulfed it fully. She taunted it ever so lightly with her lips. He gripped her shoulders tightly and squeezed her into him. Her hard taught nipples pressed into his chest and the heat of her body warmed him. He pulled her head back, and grabbed her hair, and lowered his mouth over her nipple. "Oh my God" she gasped…

Her body arched and shifted under his touch as he toyed with her breasts, moving back and forth from one to the other. Her chest heaved as she breathed deeply and groaned with delight.

A knock on his window brought him back to reality. He turned his head to see the funeral director pointing ahead. The hearse had just pulled out.

"The First Interview"

*L*eonardo was sitting behind his desk. It was a custom designed desk of superior craftsmanship—modern with clean, flawless lines constructed with a combination of deep walnut and honey colored burl woods with in-laid silver and platinum highlights. It was a work of art, much like the man himself; beautiful, rare and highly complex. The walls of his office were covered with vibrantly colored contemporary figurative paintings. The images were bold and oozed of raw sexuality.

Leonardo had three screens running simultaneously with various stock projections reflecting back at him. His crisp, white, starched shirt was buttoned all the way to the top. His thick brown hair was parted to the side and slicked back. His chiseled face was clean-shaven. Leonardo only used custom made straight razors because they gave the closest shave possible. His eyes were dark, with a depth that exposed nothing.

Leaning back in his chair, he adjusted his Ermenegildo Zegna glasses and began.

"So what exactly do you want from me, Mr. Forsythe?"

"Oh, you can call me Martin," Martin said laughingly…

Leonardo didn't move, he stared silently at Martin and waited for an answer. Martin shifted in his seat uncomfortably.

"Umm, well, you see, I'm working on a movie script of Sophia's life and I am interested in interviewing those that knew her well to help me understand who she was." Leonardo looked on coolly.

Martin stammered on, "You see, I think there was something very special about her and I want to tell her story. I get the sense that she was a woman who had a lot to offer people. And, honestly, I don't even know how I can say that since I didn't know her... I'm just following a gut feeling that I have."

Leonardo looked at him intensely as he reached down into his pocket and removed a tightly folded handkerchief and dabbed his lips. He continued to stare across the desk at Martin for a few moments and then turned and looked out the window. His eyes scanned the meticulously sculpted Japanese Garden as he made mental notes in his head. I need to change that rock formation and I still need to build that water feature.

Martin turned and gazed out the window as well. He knew better than to speak. He knew Leonardo was thinking about Sophia.

Within a few moments Leonardo turned his head and looked at Martin directly. "I don't know Mr. Forsythe, I'm a private person. What Sophia and I shared was between us and no one else. She meant a great deal to me. Her death was..."

He was not breathing... simply holding his breath in a painful pause that had no room for air. He tightened his jaw and began. "But, I would like to help, if I can. I think she deserves this." He turned his head and looked out the window again.

"I know it is a lot to ask. I wouldn't be here if I didn't think it was important. You see, I think Sophia was an exceptional human being and I think that people need to hear her story. I think she had something important to say. NO, not something to say—something to give to a lot of people...but now she can't. I believe her story can help people. I think her life carried with it an essential message that I think many, many people need to hear. I don't want to see her short life just burn away into the ether. I can't really explain it more than that. I just feel guided to do this film about her," Martin said emphatically.

Leonardo looked down at his hands as he grinded them into each other.

"That sounds like something she would have said." He smiled and then continued. "She always followed through on anything that she felt guided to do, no matter what. She did it, even if it terrified her. I've never met anyone like her, before or since. She was a very rare woman."

He paused for a moment and looked across the room at a photo of the two of them. "We were together for three years. They were the most exquisite years of my life." He walked over to his cabinet and pulled out a bottle of Glenfiddich and filled his crystal highball glass with ice and poured the carmel colored liquid into his glass.

"Would you like one, Martin?" Martin immediately took note that he had gone from Mr. Forsythe to Martin and a little glimmer of hope sprang inside. We are building a bridge he thought… "Yes, thank you, I would" he said as he smiled.

Leonardo handed Martin his glass, poured another for himself and then walked back over to his desk and sat down. He leaned his head back again and closed his eyes and took several long deep breaths. "Sophia." He said her name, barely more than the sound of his breath, spoken almost as if in a prayer, with pure reverence. His bottom lip started to tremble. He bit down on one side of it, to try and stop it.

Martin could see Leonardo opening up. He could see the softening and knew that he would share with him what he so wanted and needed to hear.

"What was she like, Leonardo? Was I right? Was there something quite special about her?" asked Martin.

With his eyes still closed, Leonardo replied. "Oh God, yes. She was like a wild and magnificent tsunami: passionate, powerful and purposeful. She annihilated me the minute I met her. Instantaneously, it was like I didn't exist. Her energy was so big, so intense and so pure. I was enveloped, but in the most incredible way. Do you know what it is like to lose yourself in another person's love?" Leonardo said emphatically.

And then he turned and looked Martin in the eye. "I'm not talking about being lost in their fear, but lost in their love. It is a precious thing. I'd never experienced that before. She was the most tender human being I have ever met."

Martin squeezed the glass in his hand and listened intently.

Leonardo continued, "She could see the beauty in anyone. And, I mean ANYONE. She taught me what love is." Leonardo shook his head as the memories started flooding into him.

"She was the most fully alive person. She took me higher and higher as we went along to places that I had never been to." Leonardo took a sip of his Glenfiddich and then looked across the room to one of his paintings.

He began again. "But to get that height, you had to draw from the very depths of your soul. She swept into my life and I was… unraveled before I even knew what happened. I don't think I will ever be the same." Leonardo looked back at Martin.

"We'd go to dinner and within minutes she'd look me in the eyes, and she'd tell me something about myself, things I'd never shared with her. Things I'd never shared with anyone." Leonardo shook his head. "She had this gift of seeing straight into you—like laser vision, right past any armor you might have and she'd blast it all open, with the most loving thing you could ever imagine a person saying.

She'd tell me how sorry she was for my pain. Pain I'd never looked at—nor had any intention of looking at. She saw it and she could feel it. And she'd rip open this wound and in the next minute she would say something else and I would feel this force of love pouring into me, like a jug of water being filled at the fire hydrant. And then it would ooze into all the little cracks in my foundation and I'd feel whole, complete in every way.

When she was there, looking at you, flooding you with everything in her being, all your pain was washed away. You were bathed in this intense feeling of love. I'd be sitting in the restaurant stripped of everything… half of me wanting to crawl up into her lap to hold onto this feeling of safety, and the other half of me wild with passion, wanting to throw her on top of the table and take her right in the restaurant. It was so intense.

"Who can live like that?… Never knowing what to expect. Never knowing where she was going to take you or how deep you were going to plunge… but the highs were so incredible you allowed yourself to let her plummet into the deepest parts of you. I loved her. I was terrified of her. And, I was addicted to her."

A knot started to form in Leonardo's throat. His hands started to twist and grind into each other again.

"Can you excuse me for one moment. I'll be right back."

Leonardo got up and walked out of the room. He walked down the hall and into his master suite. He sat down on the edge of the bed and undid the top button of his shirt. He rubbed his eyes. The tears wouldn't come. He could feel the different parts of his body responding—a dark heaviness crept into every part of his body and yet no tears would come. He lay back on his bed and closed his eyes and recalled Sophia's face … her eyes, nose and the smell of her hair, he could feel her body on him…

Lying naked wrapped within his strong protective arms Sophia felt at peace. Her body, for the first time, could fully relax into her lover. There was trust. A spiritual connection that sealed them together, that was sacred. There was a knowing that her feelings and her body were safe with Leo. She could trust him because he was man enough to love her for who she was. Her fire and passion didn't overwhelm him… he was strong enough to handle the ferocious energy that was her life force. Not all men can handle something that wild and fierce.

She looked up at him and traced his jaw line with her finger and then leaned into him and whispered in his ear. "Leonardo, if I did nothing more than lay naked in your arms this entire weekend, it would be perfect. I don't need anything more than this. To feel your breath on my neck, warm and sweet, and luxuriate in the heat of your body as it caresses mine as you make love to me over and over again. I have never wanted a man as badly as you, Leonardo. Never." She looked at him intensely and then continued,

"I love it and I hate it. I hate that I need you. I've never needed any man like this before. I don't know how to explain it. I see you or I think of you and my body ignites, my nipples get hard and I'm wet with desire just from the thought of you. I have no control over it. I am utterly defenseless. It makes me feel so vulnerable to be so … I don't even have the words."

She stroked his hair as she spoke softly. "And, I love that you bring me to that place… that you enable me to take down my walls and fully let go."

He leaned down and kissed her gently on her forehead and then worked his way down her face to her lips. Leonardo looked up at her and smiled. Her chest started to heave as it responded to his kisses.

She went on, "I love the sound of your heart beating against my back and the feel of your lips on my neck and your delicious skin against my skin. I wish I could wear you all day like a silk robe. You are so beautiful, Leonardo... your heart... your soul."

Leonardo pulled Sophia close to him, he squeezed her tiny little frame hard, and the strength of his arms said everything that his mouth could not. He ran his fingers through the long, silky strands of her hair and then pressed his face into the black mane... the sweetness of her strawberry-kiwi shampoo wafting through the passages of his nose.

Being with Sophia was effortless. It was the only thing in his life that had been effortless. Their time together flowed... it was easy, comfortable, safe, passionate, playful; there was nothing about her he would want to change in any way. She brought a peace and serenity to his life that he had never known before. That knowledge both filled him with joy and struck him with terror, at the same time.

What would he do if he ever lost her? How do you protect something so sacred? How do you ensure that it never breaks... this was a constant source of worry for him. He knew it wasn't productive to think like that, but he had never had an intimate relationship that... fed him so completely. It was like a fount that he could go to for strength whenever he needed it. But, there was some small part of him that worried, that fretted, that obsessed that he was not worthy of her. That he was not worthy of something this beautiful. It was a thought he wrestled with, constantly.

As these thoughts crept in again he pulled her closer... to hold her tight... to protect what was his. He cherished what they had together. He turned and looked at her as if to say something, but said nothing. He squeezed her tighter and then pulled her head back softly and pressed his lips down hard upon hers and kissed her with a depth of passion he had never felt before. He spoke from his heart through the voice of his body, because that was the language that he knew best. That was the language that he was fluent in.

Sophia's body responded with full passion to his touch. She pulled her head back down to look at the alluring lines and angles of his face. Her eyes sparkled as she looked lovingly into his. She pulled his top lip with her teeth and then slipped her tongue into his mouth, seducing and teasing his to come out and play so she could envelop it fully. When she had finished tantalizing it, she followed the lines of his cheekbone with alternating kisses and licks and then made her way up to his ear. She traced the outline of it with her tongue—and then continued behind his ear and down the nape of his neck. She could taste a hint of salt from his silky skin as she made her way across his collarbone and down his abdomen. His skin was a sumptuous dessert for her alone to devour.

As she made her way down to his navel she could hear his breathing getting heavy and his chest starting to heave. It gave her immense pleasure to tempt and tease his body until he begged for release. From the first moment they met, the chemistry between them had been explosive. She was a very lucky woman.

She made her way back up to his face and began to kiss his lips. "I love you, Leo." Her words seeped into his soul… softness enveloped him.

He squeezed her hard and closed his eyes … "I love you too Sophia, more than you could possibly know." …

Martin looked around the office trying to understand a little bit more about Leonardo. He took another sip of his scotch and then put the glass down on a crystal coaster that was on the desk. He peered into the bookcase across the room and saw a photo of Leonardo and Sophia at the beach. The frame was black with sleek lines. It matched the room perfectly. He got up, walked over to it and picked it up. They were a beautiful couple, he thought. He stared down at Sophia for a long time.

He had met so many fascinating women in his career, but Sophia was different than any of the thousands of women he had ever known or had the pleasure of working with. The first time he saw the slightest hint of this… and he didn't even know what to call it… was when he had gone to a Reiki Practitioner that a friend had suggested he try when his back problems had become debilitating. Desperate not to have surgery, Martin agreed.

That woman had a small piece of what Sophia had, but by no means nearly as powerful. He remembered distinctly the visceral reaction he had had to the practitioner. It was immediate. It was a connection; unlike any he had ever had with another person. Not romantic, in any way… it was hard for him to describe… a pure-connection and lightness of being… an immediate trusting…

He got frustrated whenever he thought about it because he did not have the vocabulary to put into words what he had experienced. And he was all the more frustrated because he knew, some where deep down that this connection … this thing he could not describe… was deeply profound. Martin put the picture down and walked back across the room to take his seat again. He didn't want Leonardo to think he had been snooping. He didn't want to breach his trust with Leonardo in any way. He knew that Leonardo had tremendous gifts to share—insights into Sophia—and he wanted to protect the sanctity of that relationship.

Martin sat up as he heard Leonardo's footsteps coming down the hall. He took one last sip of his drink just as Leonardo entered the rom. "I'm so sorry, Martin. I just needed a moment. Is there any way that we could finish this up another time? I've got quite a lot on my plate at the moment and I need to get back to work." Martin stood up immediately. "Yes, of course. I don't want to be a bother. Thank you so much for what you have already shared."

Martin put out his hand. Leonardo reached out his hand and shook it. "I'm glad to be of help. Call me next week and we can finish things up."

"Will do."

Martin smiled and said, "I'll let myself out."

"No, not at all. I'll walk you out." Leonardo led Martin out of his office and down the hall.

"Clearing Out"

Claudia sat Indian style on the floor of Sophia's apartment. Serene, sophisticated—a temple to white… espresso stained bamboo flooring peaked through from underneath her white-suede rag-rug, which framed it beautifully. There were two over-sized white velvet couches with a combination of large ice blue satin and small white chenille pillows. The walls of the room were a crisp, clean white and there were two large paintings of white and blue orchids hanging over one of the couches. The blue in the pillows matched perfectly the blue in the orchids. The paintings were sensual and seductive. The delicate petals invited you inside their softness, into their sexuality. Claudia sat on the floor amidst several boxes. Her mascara had long since disappeared with all the tears she had shed as she went through Sophia's things. She was listening to one of Sophia's CD's, a guitar player named Ben Howard. Claudia had never heard him before. She loved his music. His lyrics seeped deep down into the marrow of her soul.

She picked up the long stemmed and bulbous wine glass and took a sip. She smiled. "Delicious," she whispered. Sophia always had great taste in wine, she thought, as the doorbell rang. She slowly pulled herself up from the floor and walked to the door and opened it. "Hi," said Finn. She gave her best smile and whispered "hi." He stepped inside. "I brought Chinese."… He said with a smile…

"You always think of everything, Finny."

They walked into the kitchen and he put the bag down on the counter. He could tell she had been crying. "Pretty rough?"…

She nodded her head slightly. He took her in his arms and squeezed her hard and patted the back of her head. There were no words to say; his hug said everything there was to say.

Claudia sobbed a sigh, "I just miss her so much. We talked almost every day." He listened in silence.

After a moment she looked up, "Would you like a glass of wine?"

"Sure, I'll get it, go sit down and I'll make us up some plates."

"Thanks." She smiled as she took a seat at the dining room table.

Finn opened the small wine refrigerator and pulled out the half empty bottle of Isla Negra Sauvignon Blanc. He grabbed a glass from her cabinet and poured. He swirled it for a moment, placed his nose slightly into the glass and took a whiff? "Nice," he said, and took a sip.

"Yeah, it is really a great bottle. I was thinking before about how many great wines she had turned me onto."

Finn shook his head in agreement. He put the glass down on the counter and pulled out the pork lo mein, chicken and broccoli and two bowls of egg drop soup. He put together the plates and the two bowls of soup and brought them over to the table.

"Thanks so much. I haven't eaten anything today... just some coffee at breakfast and then the wine. I've lost 8 pounds."

He reached over and rubbed her hand and then gave it a tight squeeze before releasing it. Claudia picked up her fork and started to pick at the broccoli. Finn looked around the apartment as he ate.

"It's weird being here without her."

"I know," said Claudia. "It's funny the things you start to remember. I was sitting on the floor going through all her financial papers and all of a sudden I had this flash of when we were kids. It was summer vacation and Mom was in the house and Dad had already passed away. I was out in the street with her and I had put her on my bike and was teaching her to ride it. I loved that bike. It was Pepto-Bismol pink with big white and purple flowers on it and it had one of those long banana seats; it was something straight out of the Brady Bunch." She started to laugh.

"I swear it had taken me weeks to learn how to ride and I had bruises and a big cut on my knee. I would get one or two pedals and then lose my balance and fall off or run into Mrs. Edmonton's hedges. I swear to God, Finn, she got it the first go around. She had an incredible sense of balance and within 10 minutes she was riding with no hands. No Hands…I couldn't believe it. I was there to teach her how to ride and within minutes she had already surpassed me. I couldn't ride with no hands.

"She had pigtails in her hair with these little pink plastic balls on the bands, and her pigtails were completely crooked. She had large patches of hair hanging down out of them on each side in the back that she had missed. Mom had offered to do it for her, but she insisted on doing it herself. She looked so cute." Claudia was smiling as she remembered Sophia's pigtails.

"I can just imagine. I think you were really lucky to have had such a close relationship. I wish I had that with my brother, but we just don't."…

"Claudia looked at him. "It's never too late, Finn. Never"…

He looked up at her… "Yeah, I guess you're right."

She took a bite of the lo mein. "Wow, that's delicious. I don't know the last time I had Chinese."

"Me neither I don't really have a great place near me. And no Chinese is better than bad Chinese." He laughed.

"So what are you going to do with all her stuff?"

"I'm going to take a few things and donate most of it. I think she would have wanted that. I don't really have room for anything. Her artwork, I am going to divvy up and give as gifts to some special people. I'd like you to pick a painting you'd like. I'd love for you to have something special from her. You know how much she loved art."

Finn shook his head slightly, "yeah." "Are you going to keep any?"

"Yes, I think I want the orchids." "Good choice" said Finn. "They are really beautiful." "I think so too. I kind of look at them and think… I'm one orchid and she's the other." She smiled and closed her eyes as tears welled up in her eyes.

"That's beautiful Claudia… Which one do you think your Mom would like?"…

"I'm going to ask her, but I'm pretty sure she wants the nude figurative in her office by Henri Asencio. I think she got her love of art from my Mom."

"Yeah, I think you're right. How is your Mom doing?"

"Eh… she's having a rough time," said Claudia.

Finn looked at her and nodded his head. "I'm sure."

Claudia turned and looked at Finn. "Do you know which piece you might like?"

"Are you sure, Claudia? Seriously, that is so generous of you. I don't need anything. I don't want to take something you or you Mom might like."

"Finn, I'm serious. Mom and I don't have room for all her art and I would like to give them to those who were closest to her. I'm going to give one to Leonardo, Tristan and Antonio as well. You were all very important to her… and you all played such important parts in her life at different stages."

Finn smiled. "Do you think she ever would have gotten married, Claudia?"

"I don't know. I honestly don't know. I know she had mixed feelings about it. I know she wanted to be a mother. I do know that."

"Have you asked any of them which paintings they want?" "No, not yet. I wanted to give you first pick."

Finn smiled. "Well, I love this sketch she had by Francois Neilly. It's in her bedroom."

"I know which one it is. She loved that. It's yours, honey, take it." "I want you to have it, Finn."

Finn closed his eyes in gratitude "That really means a lot." He put his fork down and wiped his eyes. He sat in silence unable to say anything. Claudia rubbed his forearm for a few seconds.

"I know. I know." She got up and went into the kitchen and grabbed the bottle of wine from the refrigerator, went back to the table and poured herself and Finn another glass. They finished up dinner and then brought their plates into the kitchen. "Okay, what can I do to help?" said Finn.

"I have some boxes in her office. Would you mind boxing up her books. I'm going to donate them to the library. I've already gone through and taken what I wanted, feel free to do the same as you box them up. "Okay, sounds like a plan." Finn walked out of the kitchen and into her office. He grabbed one of the boxes and headed to the bookcase.

"Haunted"

The paint chipped, sun bleached wooden planks of the park bench were pressing hard into his lower back. A pain was shooting down his right leg. He had been there at least three or four hours staring out at the pigeons. He watched them scramble as he would throw them a handful of food. It was a great distraction. He kept trying to focus on the sound of the water spraying from the fountain to block out the terrible thoughts that kept pushing their way into his head. All the while holding the pink nylon bracelet in his left hand, rubbing his thumb back and forth over the braided folds. He hadn't slept since the accident. He would roll around his bed all night trying to push the images out of his head. Nothing worked. It was a movie that was stuck in a loop in his head and it would give him no rest, this nightmare replayed itself over and over, hour after hour, night after night. He had tried meditation tapes, melatonin and then finally prescription sleeping pills... but nothing worked. He couldn't get her blood-splattered face or those horrific gurgling sounds out of his mind. He wrestled daily with the idea of going to the police and confessing everything. Then he'd think back to what she said, "go... go now"... she didn't want him to be caught. But why? He kept asking... Why didn't she want me to get caught?

He rubbed his tired, swollen eyes and looked down at the pink nylon bracelet again. Tears pooled in his eyes, again. He'd been crying for days. He hadn't been able to eat. The thought of food made him sick. How do I live with this? How do you move on from something like this? He had never been an especially religious man but at the moment with darkness engulfing his soul he found himself being pulled to his Catholic roots. Across the park, just beyond the fountain, was a church.

It looked so welcoming with the wisteria winding up the sides of the old stone building. The purple flowers looked soft and gentle. He'd been trying to work up the courage to walk in to the Church since he got there. Every time he stood up to walk over, he would be overcome with fear and start to hyperventilate and sit back down. He had not been in a church since he was probably 15 years old. He'd been an alter boy.

"That was a lifetime ago," he said softly. What would he do in there anyway? Pray? Who would he pray to? What would he say?

In the darkest moments of his life when he had prayed to God for help... there came no help. No lifeline. No answers. Just pain. So why would he set himself up for more pain? Why would he get his hopes up that this time things would be different? No... all you ever have is yourself to rely on.

He could feel the anger rising in his chest; the feelings of betrayal from a GOD that had abandoned him. Just like everyone else in his life had.

He squeezed the pink nylon bracelet hard, as if he were pleading with Sophia herself ... Help me... help me understand ... help me get through this.

As the questions flooded his head, his breathing became shallow and the muscles in his chest tightened again. He saw a policeman on the other side of the fountain. His pulse quickened and his chest began to constrict...

Maybe this is a sign... maybe this is what I'm supposed to do?

Oh shut up, you're not going to do anything. You can't just throw away your life because of an accident. It was an accident. You didn't mean to hit her.

The voices argued in his head back and forth as the film in his head started to replay the day again. He saw the odometer and remembered the warning thoughts he'd had to slow down, but ignored. He clenched his fist that was holding the bag of pigeon feed and slammed it down against his thigh...

"Why the hell didn't you listen?... You knew you were going too fast." He muttered to himself.

He remembered why he'd been so mad and the same familiar feeling erupted in his stomach... the anger, the rage. He slammed his fist down again against his leg and the plastic bag burst and the pigeon feed went everywhere. God damn it, he muttered. Within seconds, pigeons were surrounding him attacking the wild spray of feed. He looked at the innocent birds scampering around and cried hard and deep as they moved about his feet. It was one of those soul-clarifying cries where the moans and sobs came from the deepest recesses of a scarred and bloody soul. It was a gasping, throaty, sobbing. He didn't think he'd ever allow himself to cry like this. Drowning in the depths of his emotional tidal wave, he never heard the little girl walk over.

She looked about 5 years old, with perfect blonde ringlets and a splash of freckles across the bridge of her nose. She was wearing a yellow dress with plaid fringe and a large bee on the front of it. She tapped him on the leg. He looked up and saw the look of concern on her face as she reached over and handed him a daisy and gave him a warm smile. A lump quickly filled his throat and new tears began to stream down his face. These were tears of a different sort. These were tears of love and gratitude for being on the receiving end of something so tender. It took him a few seconds to be able to speak… finally he mustered…

"Why thank you, sweetie," as a smile inched across his face. She looked up at him innocently…

"You're welcome. Daisies are my favorite flowers. My whole room is filled with daisies."

"Well you must have one nice Mommy to fill your room with daisies like that."

She blushed and giggled as she played with the ruffled hem of her dress. "Well, I better get back to my Mommy."

She flashed him one more beautiful smile before she turned and ran back across the park to her mother who had been watching. He looked over at them for several minutes exchanging hugs and laughing before they turned and walked off out of the park.

He looked down at his daisy and counted the petals… 47 soft white petals and a velvety yellow center, he thought. It was the most beautiful flower he had ever seen. He lifted the flower up to his nose and inhaled… it was a sweet scent. He smiled for the pure beauty and softness of innocence. He took the flower and held it to his chest, closed his eyes in thankfulness for the moment of solace.

"*Reminiscing*"

artin was sitting in the leather booth staring into his glass. The ice was crackling and the gold liquid glistened from the light of the chandelier above. He had that same familiar feeling in his stomach... the same feeling he got before each interview: tenseness, nervousness. He felt incredible pressure to make sure that he captured the true essence of Sophia. He'd worked under intense financial and scheduling pressures, but this was different... they were purely pressures of the mind... this was a pressure of his soul. A nagging, driving, obsessive need to get this right... to make a film that would truly touch people, a film that could change people's lives. Isn't that what we're here for, he thought. What is the point of all the money I have if, after I'm gone, I've left nothing of significance behind to have made life here better for others... made mankind's journey easier. Maybe this is what happens to you when you hit midlife. You can't help but start examining yourself and your life.

He'd always heard about this happening to people but, until you experience it, you really don't have a clue what it is or even how to explain it to someone.

He looked across the restaurant and found himself staring at a man at the end of the bar. The lines of his face etched in sorrow. He sat quietly by himself. He didn't watch the game, he didn't chat with the bartender. He simply sat staring into his drink. You could tell he'd been a handsome guy but the hardness of the years showed on his face, etched in the hollow cheeks, sunken eyes and sallow skin.

As Martin sat observing him, he could feel a heaviness oozing into him, a sadness pooling in his lungs. He turned away from the man and reached into his suit pocket and took out his cell phone and began checking his messages. He was engrossed in an email when Tristan walked up to the table.

Tristan gave him a few seconds to observe him and then realized he was quite distracted. "Good evening, Mr. Forsythe, I hope I haven't kept you waiting too long.

Martin looked up as he lay his phone down on the table and smiled at the warm face looking down on him. "No, not at all. I got here a bit early."

"Oh, good," Tristan said, as he sat down across from Martin in the booth.

"Did you find it okay?" asked Martin politely.

"Perfect… GPS is a wonderful thing! Good for me, too, since I tend to be terrible with directions." Tristan laughed.

"This is my favorite restaurant. I've been coming here for years. It just feels like home. I can't tell you how many films have been hashed out at this table. I've been coming here so long they have basically given me my own table. Got to admit, I do like that! One of the perks of being a loyal customer for over a decade! He laughed.

"But, honestly, this project is different from anything I've ever done before. I feel as though I have a certain responsibility to use the resources that I have to make a difference. Not so much that it's about me, but that I use my gifts to make a positive impact in the world, if you know what I mean."

Tristan nodded his head in agreement. "Yes, I know exactly what you mean. I've been there. It's a pretty powerful place to be. I'm sure you will find a way to say and do what you feel you need to do. Just keep listening to your gut."

Martin looked over at Tristan. He was glad that he understood so well what he was going through.

"How can I help you, Mr. Forsythe?"

"Please, call me Martin.

"Well, Tristan, I asked you here tonight because I was hoping that you could give me some insight into Sophia. You see, I saw her obituary in the paper and something about it drew me in. I feel as though she had something important, that other people need, and that I'm supposed to deliver to them… that I'm supposed to tell her story. Does that sound crazy to you?"

"Very little sounds crazy to me these days. I think each of us is on our own journey and we each feel guided to do things, even when we don't fully understand why. But we trust and listen to that voice and move forward, one step at a time. I'll help you any way I can. What do you want to know?"

At that moment the waitress came over and lightly rubbed Tristan's arm to get his attention. "May I get you something to drink while you look at the menu?"

Tristan looked up at the fresh face looking down at him. She looks so young, he thought.

"Yes, I'll have a Grey Goose and club soda, please."

She smiled, nodded her head and then looked at Martin.

"How are you doing, Mr. Forsythe?"

"I'm good, Julie, thank you. Any specials tonight?"

"Yes, we have a bean salad. Very healthy for you."

"What's in the bean salad?" asked Martin.

"It's kind of like a three bean salad, but it only has two beans."

Martin squeezed his eyebrows together and a smile cracked his lips. "What two beans?" he asked quizzically.

"I don't know, I can never remember them," she giggled.

"Do you have any soup tonight?" asked Tristan. "Yes, we do. It's delicious. It's a red lentil soup, but it's green."

Now Tristan squeezed his eyebrows together and the corners of his mouth turned up. He looked at Martin and tried not to laugh.

"Ok, thanks. I'll think about it."

She turned and headed back to the bar.

Martin looked over at Tristan, "She's a great kid. A little quirky, but she's a great kid. She's from Minnesota and she is working two jobs to put herself through college. Sweetest thing you'll ever meet." He said, as he looked down at his drink and then swirled it once with a quick flick of his wrist and took a sip.

He looked up at Tristan. "I had a whole list of questions for you about her, but after listening to your eulogy, I threw them out. I figured that I should do the same with you as you did with everyone at her service—be present and fully in the moment with you and let things unfold. I thought that would be what Sophia would have wanted. Am I right?"

A warm, deep smile spread across Tristan's face… "Kudos to you Martin, you heard what I said. I'll tell ya, you learned that a hell of a lot faster than I did. That is exactly what Sophia would have wanted."

Martin could feel tears welling up in his eyes and he didn't know why. He quickly closed them and took a deep breath and tried to push them back before going on.

"Tristan, who was she? Tell me about her, tell me anything that comes to mind. Anything you think is important."

Julie came back and quietly placed Tristan's drink on the table.

"Thank you, Julie"

She smiled and nodded her head and slipped away without a word. Tristan grabbed his drink and sat silently for a moment as he rubbed his thumb up and down the side of the crystal glass.

"God, I'm not sure where to start. There was so much to her. She was a complex person. There was simplicity to her life and, yet, she had so much depth. I've never met anyone so devoted to their spirituality. It was a major force in her life. She never stopped looking inside and trying to reach that next, higher place within herself. It was a relentless pursuit, but in a very inspiring way."

Tristan looked at Martin for a moment and then continued. "People were always drawn to her, wanting to feed off her energy because it was so powerful and pure. And, you could definitely feel it immediately when you met her. It poured out of her."

Martin looked at Tristan intently "I felt that energy you are talking about."

Tristan's eyebrows furrowed, as he looked at Martin confused.

Martin could see his confusion and tried to explain. "What I meant was, I felt it—I mean I felt her—when I saw her photo. That energy you are talking about came through in her photo, it pulled me right in."

Tristan's eyes flashed recognition and he shook his head. "I see."

Martin continued, "From everything that I have been hearing about her, she seemed pretty fearless."

Tristan started to laugh. "Ha-ha, I certainly thought she was, and I'd tell her that. But she'd adamantly deny that she was. She said she was full of fears but had trained herself to dive into them anyway."

Martin nodded his head unconsciously as he listened.

Tristan continued. "And, she did. She would rip open her deepest wounds and head straight into the darkest things that she had experienced and she'd find the good, she'd find some way to look at that terrible thing in a positive way. It was both inspiring and scary because you can't be with someone like that and not have some of it rub off. You can't help but find yourself looking at your own shit and it's not pretty and it sure as hell isn't comfortable."

Tristan laughed and lifted his glass and took a sip as he turned and looked out across the restaurant as he spoke.

"And, she lived her life at the edge, all the time. She was always doing things that scared the crap out of her and dragging me along with her."

Martin interrupted, "So you didn't want to do them with her?"

"It's not that I didn't want to do them. It's that I never would have thought to do them. She'd never force me to do anything, but her enthusiasm for whatever the hell she was doing was so infectious, I'd find myself doing the craziest things. I had the worst fear of heights when I met her... we jumped out of planes, repelled, bungee-jumped, crazy stuff. If you had told me that I would have done any of those things in my life, before I met her, I would have told you that you were out of your mind. But, I did them. And I did them because of her. I can't even imagine how different my life would be right now, had I not met her. The impact she made on me and the life I have now, it's incredible."

Martin was absorbed in thought when Tristan had finished... he was processing everything he had heard. He took a sip of his drink and then looked up at Tristan.

"I noticed her service wasn't at a church or a temple. What were her religious beliefs?

Tristan smiled. "She didn't believe in organized religion. She had been raised Presbyterian but walked away from that in her teens. She had explored a lot of different religions. But, in the end, she felt organized religions were something that divided people and she was all about bringing people together. She used to say, "the minute you say I'm a Christian or I'm a Jew, you immediately draw boundaries between yourself and that other person. But when someone says they were spiritual... well, that had no inherent divisions because a Jew could feel spiritual and a Christian could feel spiritual.

Her religion, honestly, was love. She didn't believe in going to church on Sunday; she went to a homeless shelter or a food bank instead. She was love in action, literally.

Martin interjected, "that's beautiful, but not so easy all the time."

Tristan laughed. "No doubt. And don't get me wrong, Sophia was just as flawed as any of us but what set her apart was how hard she tried every day to be better and evolve. Like I said, I've never met anyone that devoted before. I've met religious people who were devoted to, say, the Bible or the Torah... but they were committed to reading it or going to services. Her devotion lay in her continual focus, to own every inch of her behavior, admitting when she was wrong and striving to rise above her ego. She took 100% responsibility for everything in her life and she looked at every conflict, big or small, as an opportunity to grow from it."

Martin watched Tristan and when he grew quiet, Martin spoke.

"I read this article a while back, when I was sitting in a practitioner's office waiting for my session. It talked about something called Soul Contracts—the idea that we come into this world having made certain agreements about what our soul is here to learn, in this lifetime. That we have soul contracts with different people who come into our life to teach us specific lessons, and that one of the most valuable things about our relationships is that we learn to rise above the day-to-day of a relationship and figure out what lessons the relationship was meant to teach us. Do you believe in that?"

"Yes, very much so," said Tristan.

"So what lessons do you think your relationship with Sophia was meant to teach you?".

Tristan looked at Martin for a few moments, holding his eye contact, and then took a deep breath and sighed it out...

"That is a question I have pondered for a long time now. Sometimes it seems the lesson changes or maybe—that there were multiple lessons with one over-arching theme; that theme being—fear. That fear can and will destroy everything you love, if you don't keep it in check, if you let it rule your life."

Martin watched Tristan closely as he spoke. "I think there were a lot of applications all with respect to fear." Tristan shook his head up and down slightly as he said that.

"That's a pretty powerful lesson. And, you said that you did so many things that you were afraid of... all that crazy sky diving and stuff. So that was a great lesson, right?"...

Tristan shook his head slowly in agreement. "Yeah, it is a great lesson. The only problem was that it took me losing Sophia to learn it."

Martin looked confused. "What do you mean? Why did you guys break up?"...

Tristan took the last swig from his glass and then looked over to Julie who was over by the bar and tilted his glass to let her know he wanted another one. Martin turned his head and lifted his glass as well. She nodded back at both of them and within a few minutes she was serving them their drinks.

There was silence as Tristan gathered his thoughts before he continued. Martin knew better than to speak. He knew the importance of giving Tristan time.

"Sophia left because there were things she wanted and needed from the relationship that I was unable to give her." Tristan squeezed his fist around the glass and bit down on his lip. "She was a very emotional woman. She wanted and needed emotional connection." He stared down into his glass. "I couldn't do it. I had a pretty bad breakup before Sophia and I got together. It left me pretty raw. And I had a thick wall around myself and no matter how much Sophia tried to get me to take it down and let her in, I couldn't.

And the worst part is, I knew I'd lose her. I knew what she needed and I knew she'd eventually leave if I couldn't give it to her... and she finally did."

Martin looked at Tristan. He could feel Tristan's regret. It was palpable.

"Do you know how awful it is to know—absolutely know, that you lost an incredible woman like that because you were too chicken to step up to the plate and give her what she needed?"

Martin nodded his head as he watched Tristan struggling to speak.

"I was a mess… part of me wanted to hate her for rejecting me, but the other part of me knew that she deserved to have it. She simply wanted the same level of intimacy she gave me. She wanted—as good as she gave. How can you blame someone for that? There was no one to blame but myself. She gave me ample time to come around—but I wouldn't budge. My fear kept me paralyzed.

"I think some part of me was in denial, thinking she might stay, that she might love me enough to stay even though the relationship wasn't giving her what she needed. I just kept shoving the whole fucking thing in a box hoping it would go away. Denial is a brilliant strategy. I wouldn't recommend it."

Tristan picked up his glass and took another swig and then slowly put it back down on the table. He looked up at Martin and continued.

"One afternoon she came back to the apartment after returning from a spiritual retreat. She was so excited, she had had an incredible breakthrough and she wanted to share it with me. During her retreat she had taken an afternoon and gone on a hike up a mountain and sat on this overlook and written me a love letter. It talked about all the reasons she loved me, and this lovely vision she had for our future. She owned up to every fear or wound she'd ever had that she thought might have kept us from having this beautiful intimacy. She read me the letter out loud when she got back. She was sitting on the bed with tears in her eyes and when she finished, she was waiting for me to respond. My heart was racing and I was frozen. I didn't know what to say. I didn't know how to respond.

I finally looked up at her and said, "that's beautiful."

And then I got up and walked out. I was terrified she was going to ask me how I felt and that she'd expect me to share what I was feeling. I went down to my office and started working.

When I came to bed she was asleep. The next morning when I came down stairs she was sitting at the kitchen table weeping. Her eyes were red and swollen.

She looked up at me and said simply. "Tristan, it's over. I can't go on like this any more. I might as well be alone. I am alone. You won't let me in and I'm tired of being kept out in the cold."

My worst nightmare had come true. My years of living in denial had caught up with me. She broke and there was nothing I could do. It was over.

Tristan was holding back the tears. "I still love her and I think I always will. Regret is a terrible thing, Martin, a terrible, terrible thing. It haunts you and it never goes away."

Martin looked over at Tristan. He could feel the pain etched in Tristan's face. Martin looked down into his glass; he sucked the air through his teeth and then swallowed hard against the lump that was in his throat. His voice cracking as he spoke...

"Yes, yes it is. It is a terrible, horrible thing, a ghost that keeps visiting you night after night."

There was a long, silent pause as both men sat there.

Finally, Martin spoke. "I think this is about as much as I can absorb for one night. That was a lot of stuff to take in. Would you be open to meeting with me again, to talk some more?"

Tristan blinked back his tears and looked up at Martin. "Of course, whatever you need. I think what you are doing is great and I believe that you are right, I think if you do this right, it could help a lot of people. Sophia would have loved that."

"On The Edge"

S tanding at the bottom of the cracked steps of the little church he stared down at a clump of black and white bird shit that had calcified on the slate. His heart was thumping hard against his chest. It hurt. He was hurting. He'd been standing there for almost five minutes. His legs wouldn't budge. It was as if they had calcified to the slate, just like the bird shit. He reached into his pocket and pulled out the familiar pink nylon bracelet. He held it in his open palm. He choked back the tears and then squeezed his hand tightly around the bracelet. He swallowed hard and then stormed up the stairs like a soldier taking a bunker and walked into the church before he could change his mind.

Once inside the vestibule, he took a long, deep breath and slowly let it out. He took two more breaths before he stepped inside, first looking down the center aisle, then up at the alter, and then scanning the pews from left to right. There was no one in the church. He sighed and whispered a little thank you to whoever or whatever might be listening.

He walked in further and dipped his hand into the sculpted ivory Holy Water font and then genuflected. Slowly, he made his way up the aisle as he looked at the paintings hanging on the walls. The sun shone through the stained glass windows and colors bounced off the crème-colored walls. It was beautiful, he thought. It bathed the church in warm, soothing color. When he reached the third pew from the alter, he stopped and slid his way in, moving halfway down the pew until he sat down on the wooden bench. He looked around silently and took another long deep breath.

I don't think I ever remember breathing this much, he said to himself, and then thought, now what?

A voice inside answered... Just keep breathing—relax and keep breathing. You're doing great.

He looked over and counted all of the candles that had been lit in prayer, 27 candles lit out of 72. He counted out the six rows of 12 candles. For a fleeting moment, he thought about lighting a candle and then shook his head. Don't be stupid. Prayers don't work. Remember, you tried that. You're here for something else.

He looked up at the statue of Mary and followed the beautifully sculpted lines. He noted the color of the paint and the various chips, cracks and imperfections. There was something mysterious about an old church with cracked statues and melted candles. He thought of all the people that had prayed to that statue hoping for a miracle. He'd never thought of himself as a cynic, more of a realist, probably.

He had mixed emotions, sitting in the hard wooden pew. Half of him was deeply grateful to be sitting there, and half of him scolding himself for being weak, scolding him for needing something or someone to help him get through this.

Haven't you learned anything from all you have been through? The patronizing voice in his head droned on. All you ever have is yourself.

He pushed the self-attacking diatribe out of his mind and looked over at the alter, his eyes taking in the ambiance, the pulpit and the presidential chair. He remembered his childhood days as an alter server in his small church back in Des Moines when he was ten.

That was a lifetime ago. What a mixed bag of shit that was, the unapologetic voice ranted on in his head.

He thought back to all the years he struggled, trying to get as far away from all of that as possible. It would take him over 50 years before he would finally realize that you can never escape, that no amount of money, no amount of fame or success can ever take you away from your past, because your past is you. You either find peace with it or you kill yourself trying to run from it. He closed his eyes and leaned back in the pew.

As he continued to let the air fill his lungs and then release it slowly, he could feel a sense of peace washing over him. As he felt his body relax further and further, he started to cry. Within a short time, he was sobbing uncontrollably. Years of pain, anguish and struggle came flooding out of him. Having no strength left to hold it in any longer, he let it go and allowed himself to feel whatever was coming up from the darkest parts of his soul. He held back nothing.

He cried for all the wounds of his childhood. He cried for the heartbreak of his adolescence and for all the broken dreams of his adulthood. Memories from every part of his life were flashing through his brain. Like a trailer for a documentary film of some tortured soul, the images unraveled in his head.

He wanted to feel sorry for himself. He wanted to wallow in his pain. He wanted to nurse his wounds, which had gone unattended for so many years. His body exhausted, from years of keeping this poison balled up in a box and refusing to acknowledge it, refusing to honor how he felt. After years of restraint, he had nothing left to hold it in. No control whatsoever at keeping it all stuffed down. It flooded out of him, like a water main pipe that had burst and was flooding out into the streets and spraying everywhere.

His body relaxed further into the seat as the weight of the darkness gushed out. He was soul-tired, the kind of tired that takes decades to accumulate. Bone. Fucking. Tired.

He was lost in thought when the sound of voices in the vestibule brought him back to reality. Three older women entered and sat in the back pew. Within a few moments, several other people entered as well and seated themselves in the back pews. Is it time for a service? he wondered.

A priest came out of a side door and walked to the back of the church. He stared back at the confessional door for some time. In a few moments the first of the elder ladies got up and went inside. He couldn't bring himself to stop looking at the door. He turned his head around and took another deep breath. He looked down at the pink nylon bracelet.

The voices started arguing in his head.

"You are not fucking going in there! Don't even think about it. Priests have an oath. They are sworn to secrecy. They can't say anything to anyone… I don't give a shit about some fucking oath, you are not going in there. You are not telling him or anyone else. So just fucking forget about it." The voices screamed on in his head.

The door to the confessional squeaked, as the old woman came out. He turned his head and watched her hunched figure slowly, awkwardly make her way back to the pew.

The woman next to her on the bench got up and made her way back to the back of the church. He saw the rosary beads draping from her closed hand as she opened the door and went inside.

The woman who had just returned from confession was kneeling down now in prayer, working her way through her rosary beads and moving them one by one into her other hand as she made her way through her penance.

He turned his head back to the front of the church. He slid down off the seat and turned down the kneeler and then knelt down to say something. He clasped his hands together and closed his eyes. I don't know exactly who or what I'm praying to right now. I don't know what I believe at this point. I want to believe in You. I want to believe in something. I want to do the right thing. I'm just so confused right now and I feel so terrible about what I have done. I never meant to hurt that woman.

He started to sob again silently as he squeezed his hands together in grief and remorse. Finally, he finished his prayer in silence and then got up and genuflected and then slowly walked down the side aisle and out of the church.

"Reflections"

*H*is shirtless chest glowed from the light of the fire. Sitting on the soft, velvet couch in a loose pair of black meditation pants, Tristan stretched out his long, lean, legs onto the grey footstool. A white gym towel lay across his ripped abdomen. He was hot, sweaty and breathless from his hour-long Qi-Gong workout. He had grabbed a Corona as he was sitting down. The bottle was perspiring in his hands.

He gazed into the embers of the fire watching the colors moving before his eyes. The chilly, ice blue merging and toying with the orange, yellow and white flames as they danced before his eyes. Fire was so seductive he thought. It was graceful, fluid and purifying. It purified everything in its way… burning away the old until it is an ash ready to be blown away with the wind.

He remembered all the nights he and Sophia had spent sprawled out in front of this stone fireplace making love and talking about all of their plans. He raised the bottle to his lips and took another sip. He looked over and saw the crystal snow globe that Sophia had bought him sitting on the coffee table. He leaned over, picked it up and started twirling it in his hands…

Sophia and Tristan had just finished ice-skating in Rockefeller Center and had headed into a tiny, family-owned Italian Restaurant for dinner several blocks north. Once inside, he had gone to the bathroom to wash his hands and when he returned he found this beautiful crystal snow globe sitting next to his drink. It was a work of art. It was hand-blown glass and on the inside it looked liked hundreds of tiny colored balloons floating through the air. When you flipped it upside down and the snow cascaded down all around it, it was simply magical.

He flipped it upside down several times before looking up at Sophia. "I love it."

He turned it upside down once more and then placed it in front of her and then leaned over the table, looked her in her eyes sweetly to say "THANK YOU" and then gave her a warm, soft, tender kiss on the lips. He sat himself back down and looked over at her.

She was looking at him and smiling. Tenderly. Silently. He could feel the love pouring out of her eyes and oozing out of the pores of her body. When Sophia loved you, it was unlike anything else in the world. She was intense. Everything about her was intense. When she loved you, you felt it. Her love descended upon you like waves in an ocean, bathing you, caressing you, enveloping you.

Looking at her across the table he had a rush of emotion. He got up and came over to her side of the small booth and slid in next to her. He put his arm around her, turned her face to his and then leaned in and kissed her left eye lid and then kissed his way down to her ear and whispered, "You are so beautiful Sophia."

He turned her face and he looked into her eyes. "Every part of you is etched with beauty and radiance. You bring so much joy into my life. I want you to know how much you mean to me and how lucky I feel for what we have."

As Sophia looked deeply into his eyes, the tears were sliding down her cheeks. Her lips were wet with tears as they kissed the sides of his mouth and then slowly made their way all around the edges before she plunged her tongue between his lips. He pulled her shoulders in tighter to him as she seduced the inside of his mouth. He could feel his entire body growing hot.

The laughter at the next table broke them out of their intoxicating embrace. Tristan brushed her bangs aside and kissed her forehead.

"We'd better order, we still have to drive back and it will be at least two hours once we get the car and that will probably take us almost 45 minutes, with how insane the City is tonight."

The waitress came and they ordered their meal. They shared everything, as they always did. The pasta was incredible, pappardelle with mascarpone and angel hair with bolognese and two glasses of Cabernet Sauvignon. The dinner was a sumptuous feast … exactly what you would expect from an old-world, family-owned Italian restaurant; it was like eating at their own home. It was their favorite restaurant.

They finished up and headed to the parking lot to retrieve their car and head for home. When the parking attendant had retrieved their car, Tristan had moved toward the driver's side to drive, but Sophia had beaten him to it.

"You have had such a crazy week my love, why don't you sleep. I'll drive. I feel like driving."

He could feel the exhaustion of the week hitting him, so he agreed. He walked around the side of the car and slid into the passenger seat. He moved the seat back, reclined it and took his jacket off and laid it over his body as a blanket. He could use the sleep, he thought.

Tristan fell asleep immediately. He didn't know how long he had been asleep, when he heard a soft voice say to him, time to wake up, Tristan. He heard the voice, but ignored it, figuring it was some part of a dream. A moment later, he heard it again. It's time to wake up Tristan…

Some part of his brain registered that this was odd. His brain was trying to wrestle with what this was, because he hadn't remembered any dream. Was it a voice in his dream telling him to wake up from a dream? He ignored it once again. A moment later, he heard it again, but the voice was much louder and more forceful. Tristan! It is time to get up.

Another part of his brain began a dialogue with this voice from his dream. I'll get up when we pull in the driveway. I'm tired. I'm not getting up.

The voice countered again. Tristan, it is time to wake up, right now.

Aggravated because he could no longer sleep due to this incessant voice, he pulled himself up in the seat and let out a frustrated sigh. He was adjusting the seatbelt, when he heard the crunching sound of gravel. He looked up to see that they were headed straight for a lake.

He screamed "Sophia" and instinctively grabbed the wheel.

As he yelled, Sophia snapped awake. She had fallen asleep at the wheel. She instinctively tightened her grip on the wheel, and they were safely back on the road.

Tristan's heart was thumping hard. His chest constricted as he looked around in silence. He didn't tell Sophia what happened. He didn't know what happened. He didn't know who woke him up. He was bewildered. He was grateful. He didn't say a word the rest of the ride home and said very little as they got into the house and climbed into bed. His brain was clicking away trying to process and register everything that happened and trying to figure out a rational explanation for what just occurred, for who woke him up and why? No matter how hard he pondered, he had no answers.

He lay in bed replaying the events in the car. Who woke me up? Was it some part of my subconscious mind? Some relative who had passed on looking after me? A guardian angel?

The questions kept coming. He tossed and turned all night, but he couldn't sleep. He couldn't get the events of that night out of his head. It was after dawn when he finally fell asleep...

Sitting on his couch fondling the snow globe in his hand, he thought back to how much had changed since that night. How far he had come and how blessed he felt for the entire journey. "Life certainly was interesting, wasn't it?" he whispered to himself.

The fire was dying out. He contemplated putting on another log and grabbing another Corona, but thought better of it. He walked over and grabbed the steel tongs and moved the logs around to extinguish the fire fully. He closed the glass doors and sat back on the couch to finish his Corona.

He took several deep breaths as he stared at the dying embers. So many beautiful memories, he thought. He looked back at the snow globe, downed the last of his beer and grabbed his towel, stood up and headed upstairs to bed.

"Finn Looks Back"

Martin was listening to Beethoven's Moonlight Sonata as he was driving along the narrow roads that led to Finnegan's house on Block Island. The road was lined with wildflowers on both sides. It looked like a shot out of one of his movies, he giggled to himself. He noticed the houses as he drove; they looked so idyllic and serene. He mused about the irony of the perfection of an image like that ... how it made one think that everything was perfect on the inside too. But, as he had learned so many years ago, behind every perfectly mowed lawn and white picket fence, lay a very real, messy normal family trying to push it out day-by-day. The myth of perfection, he smiled to himself. It's so alluring ... we all want to believe it.

As a storyteller, he had always found it interesting how no one likes to acknowledge the messiness, the dirty sludge, bloody battles and scars that inevitably unfold in families.

Perfection is a nice thought, but that is all it is, a thought, he mused to himself. Seeing the numbers 437 on the simple wooden mailbox, he turned into the driveway. It was a small, but beautifully maintained Cape-Cod style house near the water's edge. The sun would be setting soon and Martin wanted to get inside and get settled so that he might be able to enjoy it.

He grabbed his notes and rushed out of the car and up to the front door. He saw no bell, so he knocked hard to make sure that Finnegan heard him. Within a few moments, the door opened and there stood Finn. He looked neither happy, nor sad... a neutral expressionless look on his face.

"Hello Mr. Forsythe, come on in."

Finn opened the screen door and let Martin inside. The living room was decorated simply, but there was an incredible sense of warmth and coziness to it. The space felt inviting, like a warm cup of tea and hand quilted afghan from a beloved Aunt.

Finnegan gestured for Martin to sit down.

"Do you think that we might be able to sit outside? I would love to catch that sunset."

"Yes, of course. That would be perfect. I don't know why I didn't suggest it. I've been here five years and I still love them. There is something about nature that is very grounding. Finding this house on the water was an incredible find for me. I think living here has been a form of therapy of sorts."

"I can imagine," said Martin.

Finnegan brought him through the small house and out the back door onto the wooden deck. Martin put his notes down on the table and walked to the edge of the deck and rested his hands on the rail. He closed his eyes and took a long deep inhale of the salty, ocean air.

"God, I love the smell of the ocean. There is something about it that is indescribable. It's unlike anything else."

"Yeah, I know what you mean."

Can I get you a drink? I'm going to grab a beer."

"Yes, I'll have whatever you are having."

"I'm a simple man. Just an Amstel Light for me."

"That's perfect," said Martin.

Finnegan walked back inside the house. Martin looked after Finnegan for a moment and then turned his attention back to the ocean. He closed his eyes again and listened to the sound of the crashing waves against the beach, the rustling of the leaves on the bushes beside the deck and the occasional whistling of a nearby bird. He could feel the tension in his body start to lesson ever so slightly, simply from the relaxation brought about by the sounds that were seeping into him. He heard the screen door squeak as Finnegan came out with two Amstel Lights in his hand. He walked toward Finn.

"Thanks," he said, as he took the bottle from Finn.

"Welcome," Finn smiled back.

Martin walked over and sat down in a chair that was facing out toward the ocean. Finn followed him and sat down in the chair right next to it. They both looked out at the ocean.

"Have you guys heard from the police? Have they made any headway on finding out who hit her?" asked Martin tentatively. He knew it was a sensitive issue.

Finn shook his head in disgust. "No, nothing. They don't have anything. It's very upsetting."

Finn shifted in his seat, he didn't want to talk about that. He looked out at the colorful horizon. "Beautiful, isn't it?" said Finn.

Martin was staring out at the horizon. "Yes, it really is. How did you find this place?" asked Martin.

"Well, I fell in love with the island when I came to visit for a weekend. Sophia and I had come and stayed at the "1661 Inn" and something about it really hit a chord for me. If you haven't been, I highly recommend it. Wonderful place. I grew up in the Bronx... I grew up with cement... this place felt magical to me," Finn said affectionately.

"I think you're right," said Martin in agreement.

The two men looked out at the water in silence. Each knowing that the talk that would unfold would not be easy to have. Each was taking some time to honor where they were about to go.

After a few moments, Finnegan looked over at Martin. "I love what you are doing. Sophia deserves this. I think that you are right on the money, that she had something to give. I still can't believe she is gone. No matter how many times I try to reconcile it, it just seems so unjust. She had so much to share with people and now she's gone, just like that. It really makes you take stock of your life.

She always used to say, tomorrow is promised to no one. "Well, I tell ya, I believe that now more than ever. She was so big, so full of life; you just couldn't imagine life without her, without her wild, crazy, loving energy. I hope that your film will have the impact that you hope it will," said Finn.

Martin looked at him. He was silent. He felt tears welling inside him. He didn't want to cry in front of Finn. He stood up kind of abruptly and walked over to the edge of the deck. He was suddenly overcome with anxiety. He reached his right hand down to hold the deck rail and then thrust the other one into his pocket.

"I really hope that I can do this project justice. I've never done anything like this before. I don't know if you know my background, but I have only really ever done action/adventure and comedy. This is definitely way, way, way outside my realm of experience."

Finnegan sighed a laugh. "Well, then, isn't that just perfect." If there was any theme in Sophia's life it was 'stepping outside your comfort zone.' She would have been applauding you and supporting you in any way she could. She lived outside her comfort zone. She was constantly pushing herself to do what made her uncomfortable or to face the things that she was most afraid of. I learned a lot from her."

Martin could feel a full-blown panic attack coming on. His chest started to heave as he gasped for air, and his heart hurt as it pounded incessantly inside his chest. He pulled his hand out of his pocket and grabbed the deck rail.

Finnegan jumped to his feet and ran over to him. He put his arm on Martin's back and one on his arm to steady him.

"Here, let's get you back to the seat."

Finnegan maneuvered Martin back to the chair and helped him down into the seat.

"Are you going to be okay?" Martin was rubbing his chest and his eyes were squeezed tightly shut in pain.

"Do you have any medicine to take? Can I get you some water?" Finn's voice was almost shouting.

Martin said nothing as he focused his mind and tried to remember what the healer had told him to do when this happens. He repeated his mantra in his head and then out loud over and over again as he gently rubbed his chest…'inhale calm and exhale stress, inhale calm and exhale stress.'

He kept repeating the little mantra over and over. In between he struggled to take several long, deep breaths and inhaling to the count of 10 and exhaling to the count of 20. Within a few moments his heartbeat had settled down and his breathing had returned to normal. He kept his eyes closed for several more minutes as he allowed himself to fully recover and get his breath back.

Finally, he opened his eyes and looked at Finn. The look of fear on Finns face was palpable. "Are you okay?" he said softly.

It took a few moments for Martin to respond. "I'm better, thank you."

"Would you like me to get you some water?"...

"No, I've earned this beer, this week... this is fine." Martin laughed. It was that forced, chuckle-of-fear, kind of a laugh.

Finnegan remained there for another moment to make sure Martin was okay, and then turned and went back to his chair. He sat down and looked over at Martin.

"Well that about just gave me a fuckin' heart attack," said Finn emphatically.

"I'm not very good with sick people. You'd never catch me being a paramedic or lifeguard or anything that like. That stuff sends me into a panic attack."

Finnegan took a gulp of his beer and then rubbed his eyes and forehead. "That was scary. Do they happen a lot?"...

Martin looked at Finn while he shook his head in frustration. "I've struggled with them for years, but they seem to have gotten worse lately. I got tired of taking pills so a friend recommended that I try going to a holistic practitioner and she's been working on me. She taught me how to do that breathing thing. And I have to say, it really helps."

"Maybe I should learn it. I'm not the best with stress either and my temper can get the best of me sometimes. Irish curse." Finn smiled.

Martin laughed. "Well, I'm Scottish, so you don't have anything on me. We've got our own fire, too!"

Just as Finnegan laughed, a small white bird flew overhead and landed on the railing of the deck. Both men looked over at it, but said nothing. Neither wanting to interrupt the little bird. The bird pecked around in a circle, turned, hopped three times and then flew off toward the ocean.

Finnegan spoke first. "I love when that happens. There is something about watching wildlife that is ..." he searched for the word... "hypnotic—I can't explain why, it just is."

Martin looked over... "Yeah, absolutely." A few moments passed as they both relaxed in silence to the sound of the waves.

"Well, we might as well get started then. What do you want to know about Sophia?" said Finn.

Martin looked over, took a gulp of his beer and then responded. "Well, unlike the past, I seem to be going off the cuff on these interviews... the questions just seemed so formulaic. Why don't you just tell me the things that you think are most poignant about your time with Sophia."

Finnegan was looking at Martin as he spoke. When Martin finished, Finn looked down at his hands and started fidgeting with the label on the Amstel Light bottle. He was silent for a few moments as he thought about what he wanted to say.

"Being with Sophia was a pretty wild trip. Unless you have experienced her—her energy, it's kind of hard to describe. And, she is hard to describe because she was constantly changing. If there was anything that you could know for certain about her, it was that the next time you saw her, she'd have done or learned something new. She'd be talking about some unique experience or some new perspective on things. I never told her this, I should have, she would have loved it. I used to think of her like she was water in a river. She was in a perpetual state of motion. She would keep moving forward and whatever obstacle came in her way she would just go around it, over it, under it, whatever; nothing ever stopped her. She was always moving, but not in a bad way. She knew how to be still and then, out of that stillness, there would come this huge forward motion, because she had made a new distinction and she'd immediately start implementing it in her life. When you were with Sophia, you either grow with her, or you get left behind."

Finn looked up and out over the crashing waves. He picked up his Amstel Light and took a swig and then brought the bottle down to rest on his thigh.

"Sophia helped me work through some tough shit while we were together. I was a pretty angry guy. My temper was really out of control. I'm not saying I don't get angry now, but I understand anger now, in a way I didn't before I met her. And she taught me how to use that anger, how to listen to what it was trying to tell me, instead of just letting it trigger me and then I explode and have a shitload of stuff that I regret saying and doing."

Martin interrupted him, "What do you mean, she taught you how to use anger?"

Finn looked over at Martin and smiled.

"At that time, when we were together, I was working for a guy who was a real control freak. And, to be honest, I've always had an issue with authority so working for someone who was up my ass and micromanaging me wasn't exactly an ideal scenario for me. Let's just say, it provided a very fertile place for my anger to thrive." Finn shook his head and laughed in reflection.

"One day I came home from work and I was in a nasty mood, slamming shit and cursing. And I ended up picking a fight with Sophia. That was a pretty typical way I handled my anger back then. But unlike my other girlfriends who would get all caught up in it, Sophia wouldn't go there. She wouldn't engage. Which pissed me off even more, of course." He laughed again.

"She just went about her business doing her thing and nothing I said could get her going. This went on for about an hour. I kept trying to bait her into a fight. Finally, I realized that nothing I said was going to get her going, so I grabbed a beer and went out on the deck to try and relax and forget about it all. I had been sitting out there for about an hour thinking and cooling off when Sophia comes out with a glass of wine and walks directly over to me, leans down and kisses me on the forehead and says, "I'm so sorry that you had a rough day.""

"I was stunned. I honestly didn't know how to respond. I was filled with shame for acting like such an asshole and so thankful for the love that she was giving me, in spite of how I treated her. I apologized, but it didn't make me feel any better. I told her that I didn't mean to be like that."

"She smiled back at me and said she knew I didn't mean it. Then she climbed onto my lap and we sat there for a while in silence holding each other. Finally, I looked at her and asked, how did you do that?... Do what? she said."

"I came in and I was horrible to you. I was so angry, so frustrated and I needed to let it out and I took it out on you and you didn't let it bother you. How did you do that? How did you stay so calm? You didn't let it get you angry."

She looked into my eyes and shook her head as she whispered, "No."

"But how?"

"Because I know that it has nothing to do with me and if I allow you to drag me into that anger, then we will both suffer. I know you can't stand your boss and you think he is an asshole. But here is something you might want to think about, Finn. It's not your boss you're angry at. He's simply scratching an old wound of yours, triggering an old issue from your past that you have not resolved. That's how this works, Finn."

"I sat there looking at her and listening. I wanted to understand. I was sick of my anger. I was tired of feeling like I was a helpless victim to it, like a puppet that could be manipulated by anyone who came along."

Martin shook his head slowly in acknowledgement. "Yeah… I know what that is like."

Finn continued… "I sat there holding her in my arms and thought about what she said. Wondering who and what I was really mad about. I remembered a terrible fight I had with my Dad in junior high school. He was a pretty angry guy, too. As you can imagine, it was pretty ugly. We were both screaming some terrible stuff at each other and then my Dad lost it and punched me in the face. My mother was crying and called the police. It was one of those moments which changes your life."

"My father had never hit me before. I was devastated. I felt so betrayed. I wanted to hit him back but, instead, I just cried. I was angry with him for hitting me and I was angrier with myself for crying and showing him that I was upset. I was filled with rage for all the times he had never been there for me; angry for all the times he scared the shit out of my Mom and me with his violent temper. I was holding Sophia in my arms thinking about all this and tears were streaming down my face."

"I swear, I cried 30 years worth of tear's that night. I cried all the tears that I had never allowed myself to cry when I lived at home, when I lived in a constant state of fear of him. I cried for the death of my childhood, for the death of the dream I had had where you had a Dad who looked out for you, who made you feel safe. I cried for the relationship that I had never been able to experience with my Dad and had craved so deeply."

"Sophia said nothing… she sat there holding me, loving me, allowing me to shed all this pain with no judgments, no answers… She simply gave me the space to let it all out, knowing that I was safe in her arms, knowing that she didn't think less of me as a man, for crying like a little boy."

"It was one of the most powerful moments of my life. I had never before allowed myself the chance to feel all of these horrible feelings, to allow myself to acknowledge how hard it had been. She helped give my feelings a voice. It was a serious turning point for me."

"We went upstairs and Sophia and I made love that night and it was the most beautiful experience I have ever had. I felt connected to her in a way that I have never felt connected to another human being, ever. Whatever we had just gone through had removed any walls or barriers that I had up and it was—indescribable. I had no idea that you could ever feel something as extraordinary as that."

"The next morning when I woke up, I literally felt lighter. I could honestly notice a physical change in my body… a weight had been lifted. Whatever pain I had managed to release was gone and left in its place was this light, airy, spacious feeling. I could breathe, really breathe. For the first time in a very long time I could truly say I felt relaxed."

"The Confession"

He sat in the pew silently contemplating what he was about to do. His hands were hot, sweaty and trembling. He took a handkerchief from his pants pocket and wiped his brow. A burning acid was churning in his stomach. He hadn't eaten any solid food. He had only had three large cups of coffee all day. The thought of food made him want to throw up. The caffeine was hitting his empty stomach pretty hard. He just wanted to get this over with. He wanted to get this weight off of his chest. He was having nightmares and the chest pains were growing worse and worse.

He woke up that morning knowing that he couldn't take it any longer and needed to speak to someone about what he had done. The weight of the guilt was torturing him. He started to cry. He was so tired of crying. The tears, guilt and the heaviness, the pain seemed endless. He was praying his confession would bring him some peace, some forgiveness. He wasn't even sure if he would be able to remember half the prayers.

He wondered if that really mattered. He wondered if God knew if you knew the words to the prayers or if all He cared about was the feeling that you had inside. Maybe the only thing that really matters is that you truly are sorry. Fuck the prayers he thought ... who cares about the prayers. Maybe I will start donating money to an orphanage every week and donate it in her name. He began to cry even harder. He reached into his pocket and pulled out a ragged tissue.

It was a dark, sullen day and the church looked gloomy with the greyness from the outside. He was anxiously waiting for the start of confession. He was the first person in the church, although he was hoping that there would be others. He didn't think he could go first. He heard the bang of the heavy wooden door to the vestibule and a small wave of thanks ran through his body. There was someone else to go first.

He needed more time. He kept reciting in his mind how he would tell the priest. He didn't think he would be able to make it through without crying. He reached into his pocket and pulled out the familiar pink nylon bracelet. When he looked at the bracelet and felt it in his hands, he could see Sophia's face and he could feel the loving gaze she had given him. He could feel the forgiveness she had bestowed upon him as her parting gift to the world.

How does one confess to killing someone? He said silently in his head. How does one find the words to speak something so terrible? He closed his eyes and remembered the accident like he had so many times before. He was staring into her beautiful face and hearing her words "Go. Go now."

He had tried so many times to forgive himself, but how do you forgive yourself for taking the life of another human being, even if it was an accident? How does one have the audacity to say it's okay, when it's not? The muscles in his chest began to tighten. "It's not okay." The voice in his head screamed.

The priest came out of the side door and made his way to the back of the church. Within a moment of stepping inside, the old woman who had come in stood up genuflected and then turned to go into the confessional. A few moments later a number of other parishioners came into the church and sat down in the last pew to wait their turn. A short time later, the woman came out of the confessional. He looked over at her. "I'm not ready," he muttered to himself. He remained seated.

He watched as another old woman got up from her pew, genuflected and walked to the back of the church. He turned his eyes to the woman who had just come out. She was back in the pew on her knees and was just starting the rosary. He watched as she moved her way around bead by bead.

"I wonder what she is confessing?" he thought. A sweet little old woman, what could she be confessing? It's always old women at confession. Don't any old men have anything to confess? Don't men have any guilt?

He looked down at her hands again as she moved the beads one by one. I wonder how many times she has said The rosary in her life? I wonder if it helps? How many beads are on that thing anyway? How many Hail Mary's are on that thing, he wondered.

God, I wish that woman would hurry up… I need to do this. I need to get this the hell over with. He was still staring at her rosary beads when he heard the bang of the door and saw the old woman moving towards her seat. He stood up, moved to the edge of the pew, genuflected, and then slowly made his way down the aisle. He stopped in front of the door for a moment, a last pause to consider what he was about to do. He lifted the nylon bracelet to his lips and kissed it and then opened the door to the confessional and stepped inside.

"Orchids"

eonardo was the first to arrive. It was a preliminary meeting to discuss a potential investment his company was thinking of making. He sat, as he always did, exactly halfway down the long maple wood table in the corporate offices. He placed his planner down on top of the business plan that was on the table in front of him. He reached over and grabbed one of the pitchers of water and poured himself a drink. It was going to be a long, boring meeting. He looked across the table and out the window. It was a dark, gray rainy day. You could barely see anything; the windows were almost completely fogged up.

He hated rainy days. He always had. No matter what, they always made him feel heavy and depressed, even if he didn't necessarily feel that way when he woke up. He closed his eyes and rubbed his forehead. Exhausted was too light a word to describe how he felt.

His schedule had been particularly brutal lately. The company was reviewing multiple acquisitions and the due diligence process was ridiculous. Everyone had been working 60 to 70 hour weeks for the past two months. He was fed up with reading business plans. He was sick of these meetings. So much jockeying and positioning for power, everyone fighting for his or her own agenda. Office politics and bureaucracy was never a strong suit for Leonardo.

One by one his colleagues started to filter in. He didn't look up. He didn't feel like talking with anyone right now. He pulled out his iPhone and started checking his emails. He flipped through old emails rather than engage in a discussion with anyone. He had no small talk left in him right now. All he wanted to do was park his butt on a beach chair for a week and just veg—not speak, not think, not move. Just bake himself in the warm sun with the sound of the surf in his ears and relax.

The meeting started on time without any hang-ups. Mark Donovan began his overview. Leonardo looked over at him but his mind was somewhere else...

It was a cold, snowy winter morning. Leonardo had already been at work for several hours when he heard a soft knock at the door. "Come in," he called as he dialed Jim's number in Accounting. The door opened slowly and Sophia stepped inside. She was wearing a knee-length red satin jacket and black peek-a-boo pumps. Her hair was swept up on the sides with white pearl hair combs, while the rest hung down long in the back in beautiful curls. She had a small bag in her hand, which read H&H bagels...

"I brought you a little treat sweetie."

Just as he smiled, Jim answered in Accounting without Leonardo hearing.

Sophia stepped inside, did a little half-twirl and turned the lock on his door, then placed the bag of bagels down on the table next to his couch. Leonardo was watching carefully. She turned toward him, leaned her back up against the wall and undid the belt of her jacket.

"I also brought you some flowers." She smiled.

As the jacket swung loosely open you could see a burst of white come from underneath the jacket. As she inched the jacket down off of her shoulders he could see the full effect.

"I brought you some orchids"...

His head went to the top of her shoulder where the cascade of flowers started. The petals were white in the center and the column was a just a dab of honey-yellow, the lips were red and the throat was blue. Hundreds of tiny orchids cascaded down over her breasts, down past her navel, over her pubic bone and filtered off at the very top of her thigh. It was stunning against the glow of her beautiful tan, sculpted body.

Leo was awe-struck... "Is that body paint?"

"Who is this?"

"Huh?"

"Who is calling me?" said Jim in Accounting...

Leonardo realized he was on the phone and slammed it down fast.

Leonardo looked up at Sophia again. "Is that body paint?" …

She smiled and shook her head ever so slightly. "It's edible."

Leonardo could feel himself getting hard.

"Sophia you look incredible. Oh, my God"…

"Leonardo, do you know why I chose white orchids?"

He was devouring her body with his eyes. He shook his head back and forth as he said "No, why?"

"Because white orchids are saved for the most special person… the person that you love the most." She smiled. She bit the lower part of her lip as she waited for Leonardo to respond.

As he stood up, his eyes moved to the clock on the wall next to her. It read 8:25.

"Oh shit. Sophia, this is so incredible. I am totally speechless. But, honey, this is the worst day possible for this. I have a huge presentation at 9:00 and I'm not finished putting it together, but I love this. This is just … I don't even… oh, my God."

She looked at him a little sad. "Oh, I didn't know this was a bad time. I'll go"…

She looked at him with a little devilish glint in her eye. "I'm sure I'll find someone I can give these flowers to." She shot him a wicked smile.

He looked at her… "Get over here."

She started to giggle. "Well, if you're too busy. Seriously, I'll just leave."

"Get over here," he said even louder.

She smiled and slinked her way across the room.

He was standing behind his desk, staring at the delicious flowers that were showering her sculpted body. She shoved him against the wall. He gasped.

"You know my boss's office is right behind this wall, don't you?"

"Of course I do."

He could feel himself get harder. She pushed his head back against the wall, grabbed his jaw and turned his head so that his neck was completely exposed. She took her tongue and licked him from his Adam's apple up to the tip of his chin. She nibbled on the sides of his soft, full lips. She could feel his heart beating hard against her naked chest. She kissed her way up to his neck and then plunged her wet tongue into his ear, caressing it inside and out and then whispered, "tell me what you want me to do to you right now, Leo.".…

"Oh, God Sophia. You know what I want."

"I want you to beg me for it." She taunted.

He grabbed her body and picked her up and turned her around. Now he had her up against the wall. She looked to the side, indicating the wall and his boss on the other side…

"Are you going to make me scream? I've never been very good at being quiet."

Sophia reached both hands around Leonardo's head and pulled him into her. She led his head directly to her white orchid covered breast. He put his mouth on her nipple and moaned, "Ohhhh—that's so sweet"

"It's white chocolate icing, the red accents are raspberry and the blue are boysenberry." She giggled.

He lifted her ass up and slid her further up the wall. She threw her arms back and slammed them against the wall. He jerked his head up to look at her.

"Sophia!" He got even harder.

She shot him an evil smile. "Sorry."

He leaned down and kissed her hard on the lips. She pulled him close to her and she ripped his shirt out of his pants. She wanted to feel his skin on her body. She pulled open his shirt and squeezed him against her.

"I love the feel of your skin against mine…

She leaned in and started nibbling on his chest while she slid her hands around back and pushed down his underwear so that she could feel his soft, luscious ass.

"You have such a great ass."

He knew she loved his ass. He smiled with pride He had started doing extra squats when they started dating. It's her ass and he knew it. He worked hard to make sure she always had something nice to appreciate. She pulled her legs down from around his waist, stood up and then took his shoulders and turned him so that she could push him down into his chair. Then she crawled up on top of him. She kissed him deeply, all the while rotating her hips in a circular motion taunting and teasing him. She could feel how hard he was getting. She loved to drive him crazy. His chest was pounding and he was breathing heavy as she kissed him. She ran her fingers through his hair and then grabbed a chunk as she pulled his head in closer to kiss him. She gave him a long, sensual kiss, licking every inch of his mouth. She abruptly turned her head to the clock. It was 8:53. She climbed off of him.

"Well, I'd better go; your meeting is in 7 minutes," she giggled.

"What?—Holy Shit, 7 minutes."

He stared back at her in shock. He got his breath for a second and then looked down at his shirt for the first time, it was smeared with raspberry and boysenberry.

"Oh, shit, what am I going to do with this, Sophia? I don't have any spare clothes?"

She laughed as she walked across his office, picked up her red satin jacket and slipped it back on. "I just wanted to give you a little something to make you think of me today while you were in that boring meeting. We can finish this up when you come home."…

"Sophia, what the hell am I going to do about my meeting? I can't go in there like this? Holy shit."…

She looked at him calmly, smiled, and then turned the handle of the door…

"Oh, by the way… I left a clean suit, shirt and tie with your secretary before I came in."

She blew him a kiss and walked out.

"Presence"

Martin was tired. His eyes felt heavy as he drove along the slick, winding road that led to his house. He was thankful that the teeming rain had stopped. He found driving in that kind of rain to be very stressful. He didn't like it at all, especially at night. It had been a long week. He had several unsuccessful meetings with potential financiers for the movie; they were uncomfortable with Martin's storyline. "Too risky. Why don't you stick with what works," they had said.

His body was heavy and listless. All he wanted to do was crawl into bed and sleep for a few days. He started to pick up speed; he just wanted to get home.

A small dog darted out into the middle of the street. "Oh, shit," he muttered and slammed on his brakes. The car slid on the wet pavement and he started to veer sideways off the road. He squeezed the steering wheel hard and quickly guided the car back safely in the right direction. Shaken, he slowed to a stop to make sure he hadn't hit the dog. He looked in the rearview mirror. There was nothing in the road. He let out a slow, deep breath. His heart was still pounding hard.

He rubbed his forehead and reached for the half empty bottle of Acqua Panna in his cup holder.

Damn thing almost gave me a heart attack. Crazy dog. He took a few sips of water and placed the bottle back in the holder.

He put his black Mercedes back in gear and slowly started off down the road. His mind wandered back to all the various meetings he had had during the past few months involving this project and it seemed there was a tremendous resistance to funding it.

"Looks like it is time to put up, or shut up, Martin," he whispered in the silent car.

Does it matter that much to you? Are you willing to risk your own money?

His mind was flooded with thoughts.

Financing a movie can be like going to Vegas. Sometimes the one's you think will hit it huge, tank. And the one's you are sure are going to fail, become a cult classic and make hundreds of millions.

He sighed, reached over and turned on his CD player. Ludovico Einaudi's Una Mattina began playing. Within seconds of the soothing melody coming through the speakers, he could feel his body sigh with relief. He could feel the stress and tension slowly start to ooze out of his body. The muscles in his arms gradually transformed from tight, constricted pieces of wood into soft, relaxed human flesh again. He could feel them. He could feel the sensation of his hands on the leather wrapped steering wheel. He could feel the rush of blood as it moved into his fingers. He was conscious of the feel of the tips of his fingers as they guided the wheel along the winding road to his house. He noticed the bright pink flowers on the trees that were in bloom. It was the first time he had seen the flowers this season. He felt a sudden pang of pride. He didn't know why. It just seemed to bring him an odd sense of peace simply by appreciating their beauty.

Curious, he thought.

He wound his way up through the many twists and turns of the mountain road and finally reached his house at the top. He pulled the car into his long, gravel driveway. As he pulled up to the house, he stopped the car in front of the large, tiered water fountain. There was a fat, round frog perched on the second tier of the fountain. It was enormous. He had never seen a frog that big before. He didn't want to frighten it. He put the car in park and rolled down the window. He sat staring at the frog. He watched as the big, slimy frog bellowed her croaks. The water was pouring down around her and she was oblivious. She was perched like Pavarotti at center stage of Carnegie Hall with the water as her chorus.

It was incredible. Martin felt a gush of playfulness as he watched this fabulous frog. He loved it. I wonder how many times she might have been sitting here and I missed it, he thought.

I wonder what else I have missed when I wasn't paying attention? he mused in his head. The frog croaked on for quite a while before finishing her solo and then turned and jumped into the water on the first tier. She swam to the edge of the fountain, climbed up and hopped down onto the gravel driveway. Then hopped off silently into the garden. "The fat lady has sung," laughed Martin.

He pulled the rest of the way into the driveway and parked. He gathered his briefcase and jacket, got out of the car and headed to the house. He opened up the front door and reached over to shut off the alarm, placed his jacket on the table in the entryway and went upstairs. He walked into the bedroom, turned on the TV and took off his clothes, draping them on the small couch in his bedroom.

The news came on and it was consumed with the wild fires that were raging through Malibu. He stood in the center of the room in his boxer shorts watching intensely as he shook his head back and forth at the footage. So much devastation, he thought. I can't handle this right now. He walked over and switched off the TV.

He walked into the bathroom and flipped on the light, stepped in front of the mirror and looked at his face. You need to get some sleep, Martin. You are not looking so hot right now. He looked at the deep brown patches under his eyes.

When did I get so old? he whispered. He looked down at his belly. "When did I get so fat?" he smacked his belly annoyingly. He looked back at his face, again. He looked deeply into the mirror, directly into his eyes.

That's not very nice Martin. That's not going to help things.

He knew that if he continued down this path he would have a full-blown spiral. He'd start heaping everything he could think of on top of this and find every single mistake he'd ever made and spend the next hour berating himself. He held his own gaze as he continued the interrogation.

Is this where you want to go? Is this actually intelligent? Is there any way this could help you right now?

He closed his eyes, took a deep breath and then shook his head. No, not today, Martin… not going there.

He felt the dull ache of an oncoming migraine. Oh, shit... not now. Then he remembered the exercise that his friend suggested for his headaches. He walked back into the bedroom and sat down next to the wall. How the hell am I going to do this? He lay down on the floor, shimmied his legs up the wall and inched himself in closer to it as he kept his back flat on the ground. He said fifteen minutes... Martin looked over at the clock and registered the time 11:22... Okay, here we go.

He could feel his leg muscles stretching a bit. God I'm out of shape. He closed his eyes and tried to relax to help pass the time. "Just focus on some long deep breaths and before you know it, you will be done, he said to himself.

Within a short time, he could feel a burning sensation behind his knees. Shit, he sighed and shifted his legs trying to manage the pain. I've never been limber.

He opened his eyes and looked over at the clock. 11:25... Oh, Christ... he wants me to do this for 15 minutes EVERY DAY? He sighed and rolled his eyes. He did notice his back felt quite good like this. He decided to bend his knees just a tad and shimmied his butt back out a bit away from the wall. That felt much better. THIS I can do.

He smiled a little victory smirk. You ROCK!... He looked down at his body with his hairy chest, his plaid boxer shorts with a layer of fat hanging out and his pale white legs haphazardly pushing against the wall and started to laugh. He started slapping his flabby gut to the beat of Johnny Cash's "I Walk The Line"... and then started to sing the lyrics. "I keep a close watch on this heart of mine. I keep my eyes wide open all the time," all the while slapping the melody out on his stomach.

He was slapping and singing away for a few minutes before he thought about how ridiculous he must look right now and started to laugh even harder. He had a sudden flash of this in a scene in a movie. He was laughing so hard his leg slid off the wall and jerked his body as it slammed onto the floor. It felt so good to laugh. It felt like a purging of the spirit, a comic shower to wash away the hardness of day-to-day life. It had been a long time since he had laughed this hard and this deep. He was thankful. He lay there laughing for some time before he looked over at the clock... 11:58... Woohooo!!!! I made it.

He rolled his other leg down off the wall, got up, went into the bathroom and grabbed his toothbrush. He caught a glimpse of himself just as he was grabbing the toothpaste. He was smiling. He paused for a second and looked for a moment deep into his eyes and said out loud, proudly, "you've got a nice smile, Martin, do you know that?"... He gave himself a quick wink, put a quick dab of toothpaste on his brush and started to brush his teeth.

"Block Island"

innegan was sitting on his back deck having his morning coffee. He was listening to the surf rolling in and watching the gorgeous lines and colors in the sky. He loved mornings on the Island. They were so serene. Such a civilized way to start your day before the onslaught of phones ringing and emails coming in. Sitting out here, fully a part of nature, was like being engulfed in a soft sonorous meditation. The sound of the waves hitting the beach was like a sound-healing session. He could feel his body relax further and further with each crash of wave against the surf. He closed his eyes and started thinking back to his interview with Martin and the things that he had shared. He was working his way through the conversation in his head when he suddenly had a flashback of a time with Sophia…

He and Sophia were on the ferry heading over to Block Island. Sophia's seasickness was so violent she couldn't sit up. His hands softly stroked her hair while she tried to rest. He looked down at this beautiful, soft creature who was always so filled with explosive energy, was now scrunched up in a tiny ball and resting her head in his lap. He scanned the lines of her face and then traced his finger along her eyebrow. Then, he leaned down and gently kissed her on her forehead. It was a tender kiss. He could feel his heart fill with emotion as he stared down at her. Within a few moments, the ferry was pulling into the dock and the passengers started to disembark from the boat. Finn rubbed Sophia's arm… "Honey—we're at the dock, time to get up."

Sophia rubbed her eyes and slowly opened them. She blinked several times. Finn helped her to her feet and they made their way to the door.

The air had a chill and it was quite foggy. There was an aggressive wind whipping about.

As they slowly made their way down the dock toward the road, Finn could feel something special about this place. It felt like home. He looked at the colorful sign and smiled "Welcome To Block Island"... He was so glad to be here and to have this weekend with Sophia. The Inn wasn't far from the dock. They arrived within a few minutes and quickly settled into their room. Sophia decided that she needed to try and sleep off the seasickness and immediately settled herself on the bed.

"Are you sure you don't mind if I get a little sleep? I think if I rest, I will be back to my normal self by dinner."...

"Do whatever you need to do to feel better, Soph. I'm going to take a walk and get myself acquainted."

He leaned down on the bed to give her a hug.

"Thanks," she said as she wrapped her arms around him and gave him a big tight squeeze. "You're the best, Finny. I'm so happy we finally made it here. I love Block Island. It's a really special place and I think you are going to love it here."

He smiled back at her. "I can feel it already, Soph... I can ... I can feel there is something special here."

She giggled softly and kissed him lightly on the lips. "I've gotta lie down, my sweet. See you later, enjoy your walk."

He smiled back. "Feel better... be back in a bit."

He turned, grabbed the key off the table and walked out of the room. He headed down the stairs into the lobby and inquired about the best place to walk. The clerk gave him instructions and he headed out down the road.

He found the entrance to the beach just where the clerk had said it would be. He walked for a little ways and decided to sit down on the sand and look out at the ocean. He didn't want to walk, he wanted to sit and take in the ocean... this moment... this place in his life. He picked up a pile of sand and poured it from one hand into the other. He loved the feel of the grains as they trickled through his fingers. He was thinking about the conversation he and Sophia had had at dinner last night. He could not stop thinking about what she had said to him. It was so simple and made so much sense… but no one had ever explained it to him like that before…

He had been angry with a co-worker who he felt had betrayed him and lied to him. He had ranted on and on almost all through dinner as she sat listening and letting him vent. Finally, when he had nothing left to say… he paused, looked over at her and said… "So what do you think of that? Would you feel betrayed?"

She could see the wounded look in his eyes. She responded softly. "I'm sure when it was unfolding, I would probably have been taken off-center and gotten upset… but then when I calmed down and had time to cool off and think things through… I would probably ask myself this question… If someone is running a negative unconscious pattern of lying to themselves and unable to honestly acknowledge who they are and what they want and what they don't want, is it rational to expect that they would be capable of being honest with another human being? If they are unable to even be honest with themselves, how can they be honest with others? And, is it even fair to be angry with them for not being honest with you? We don't get angry with a child who has not yet learned to walk… How can we be angry with someone who has not yet learned to speak their truth?"

He looked at her in silence. He was letting her words sink in. He felt the truth of it. He felt the truth of that for himself, about his own inability to be honest with himself about certain things … things he tried to deny that he didn't like. Her words hit him, sharply. He looked over at her for some time and then spoke.

"Where do you come up with this stuff Sophia?"…

She raised her eyebrows and started to laugh. "What do you mean?"…

"I mean, seriously, where do you come up with this stuff? How do you know this?"…

"Finny, my sweet, in any situation I look at the individual who I am in conflict with and I ask myself a few questions. Is this person living a joyful and authentic life … which is usually pretty evident … and most people aren't. Then I remind myself that if they are not living their authentic life, then they are in the midst of an internal conflict that has nothing to do with me what so ever. Knowing that, how can I take it personally? I just happen to be there when the storm hits. And, if I do start to take it personally... then I stop and ask... how is this serving me in any positive way, to take their baggage and strap it to my back? That is absurd. It is totally destructive and it is not how I want to live my life...

"You have no control over what any other human being on this earth thinks, feels, says or does. The only thing you have control over is how you respond in any given situation. And if you allow yourself to be taken off your center... if you allow yourself to get angry... you have no one to blame but yourself."

He sat across the table silently staring at her. He let her words seep deep inside of him. He thought back to all of his fits of anger and the rage he had felt at various times in his life and he laughed... he laughed deeply from his gut. For the first time he saw a light at the end of the tunnel for himself. He could see a place everyone talked about called 'inner peace' and now he had some directions on how to get there.

He scooted out of the booth, came around to her side of the table and slid in next to her. He took her face in his hands and kissed her softly, sweetly on the lips, and then whispered, "I swear sometimes I think you are my own spiritual guru." Then he laughed and ran his fingers through her hair...

"My own personal guru—I'm the luckiest guy in the whole world." He leaned in and he kissed her again, deeply. A soft moan escaped from her lips.

"Upstream"

ntonio was busy wiping down the controls of his Chris-Craft Limited Silver Bullet. The streamlined 20-foot sport boat had a 270-hp drive engine and was a flawless mechanized sculpture designed for that special kind of boat lover. The Chris-Craft was for the connoisseur, for the person who paid attention to every detail in the craftsmanship. And, when it came to boats, that is definitely what would appeal to Antonio, who had always loved being on the water from as early as he could remember. He loved flying through the water with the wind hitting his face. It was one of the most incredible feelings. He found it to be his best means to relax and put the world behind him.

He looked down at the dash as he was cleaning it and remembered the first boat he had ever owned. He had only paid $1,500 for it, but it got him on the water and gave him that sense of freedom that he had come to crave. He laughed as he thought about it. The engine would smoke if he drove it too long and the seat cushions were worn, but he had loved that boat. He had saved for two years, squirreling away money while he worked odd jobs putting himself through college.

He remembered distinctly the day he bought it how proud he was of himself. He knew that day that there would be more boats ahead of him, bigger, newer, sleeker... but none would mean as much to him as this one.

In purchasing his first boat, he had proven to himself that life was simply about setting your mind to a goal and working your ass off to make it happen. That little boat gave him the certainty that whatever he decided to do, he would do it and that life was only going to get better from that moment.

He was lost in that thought when he heard steps on the dock. He turned his head and saw Martin smiling down at him.

"Hello"… He had a brown grocery bag in his arms. "I thought I'd bring a few snacks."

Antonio smiles and laughed… "Well, that was very generous of you. I have the refrigerator stocked, but we can always have more snacks."

Martin stepped down onto the boat and handed Antonio the bag of groceries.

"Thanks," he said, as he took the bag to the small refrigerator.

A gust of wind blew and Martin shuddered. "Wow, the wind is pretty fierce," he said, as he zipped up his blue windbreaker and pulled his linen baseball cap down a little tighter on his head.

"Yes, it can get quite windy. But I love it. I really love it. Some of the best memories I have ever had have been on the water."

"I bet," said Martin.

"Well, let's get on our way and then when we stop for dinner, we can chat. How does that sound?"

"That sounds perfect. I'll park my butt back here and just enjoy the ride," said Martin.

"Sounds like a plan."

Antonio backed the boat out of the slip and made his way through the marina and out to the river. He turned to Martin and said, "This is a beautiful time to come out. You'll get to see the sunset."

"It's magnificent," Martin said as he smiled. "What a great way to end my week. Thank you for inviting me out here."

Antonio nodded his head in acknowledgment and then moved the boat expertly through the water. His eyes scanned the river for any debris that might be around as many a careless driver had ruined his hull on this river slamming into a floating log that they had come upon too fast and were unable to avoid. That was not a mistake he ever planned on making, not with this beautiful work of art in his command.

Antonio felt a bit of tension in his stomach as he thought of the coming conversation with Martin. He wasn't sure what kind of questions Martin wanted to ask him about Sophia. He hadn't yet decided how much he was willing to share with him. He decided when he had agreed to do the interview that he would do it the way Sophia would have done it... to just be in the moment and share whatever he felt comfortable sharing. That was never easy for him. He always had to push himself to do those things, but what always stuck with him, over and over again, was that when he did that, he always walked away with the best feeling. He always felt at ease with how he had handled the situation, any situation. It was definitely a learned skill, though. That was for sure. And the more he did it, the easier it had gotten for him. He only wished he had learned it sooner, he thought.

He was looking way down river when he heard the subtle sounds of a seagull's wings as they gracefully moved through the air just off the side of the boat. He loved the birds and all the wildlife he got to see. It always made it that much more interesting because it was always new and you never knew what kind of interactions you might have for the day.

Martin had been admiring the stunning views of the homes that lined the riverbank. It was a remarkable setting. He wondered why he had never bought a boat.

"Maybe when I finish this film, I'll buy a boat. I think I've reached a place in my life where it is time to start enjoying myself more. I think I've earned the right to relax a bit," he said to Antonio.

"I'll tell you right now, you won't regret it. People joke about a boat being just a hole in the water you pour money into, but I think it is like an investment in your soul. How do you put a price on something like this that gives you so much pleasure? I was never a big traveler; the water was always my vacation. Everything is a matter of priorities. I'd sell my house before I'd ever sell my boat," Antonio laughed.

"If push came to shove, which I obviously have no intention of letting happen, but if it did, if I had to pick one, I'd pick my boat. That is how much I love the water."

"Have you ever had a house boat," asked Martin...

Antonio laughed. "No.... I need speed, that I'm pretty clear on." Antonio turned his attention back to the river. He started scanning the water once again and was looking upstream for his favorite spot for them to pull off.

With the gentle rocking of the boat as she moved through the water, Martin found his eyes closing in a state of pure relaxation. He was right, thought Martin. The wind in your face is incredible. He was soaking all of this in when he felt the boat start to slow and finally come to a stop.

Antonio had brought them over to a beautiful alcove on the edge of the river banks. There were huge, lush trees lining the river and there was a little family of ducks by the water's edge and several large rocks that jutted out from the shore with a large patch of green grass just beside it.

"That would make a beautiful place for a picnic," he said to Antonio.

"Absolutely. I see families there all the time on the weekends with their kids and they'll swim in this area here," as he pointed over to the left side of the alcove. "This is a great place to chat and catch a view of the sun as she sets. Would you like a beer?"

Martin smiled… "Yeah, that sounds perfect right about now."

"All right, then." Antonio walked over and grabbed two beers out of the small refrigerator and handed one to Martin.

"Here you go, sir."

Martin took the beer and started to shake his head and laugh.

"What's so funny?" said Antonio.

"It's just funny that I have never been more nervous about getting a movie project right than this one and, at the same time, I have never had this much pure relaxation during the preparation of a movie. These interviews have been pretty amazing, actually. I'm always so nervous before I get to one, but once I get there, everyone makes me feel so welcome." He paused for a second and then continued.

"Well, I guess the only one that was a little stiff was with Leonardo. Do you know him?"

Do you know him? "I don't know him personally, but I know who he is. From what others have told me, he can be a little standoffish at first, but once he gets to know you, then he loosens up a bit."

"Yes, that is what happened." Martin was nodding his head as he continued. "I just find that the time I spend connecting with those who knew Sophia so well feels so relaxed and—easy. And, each of you has been so kind to share your stories with me about her. Listening to everything that you guys have been saying, she seems like an incredible person. I feel lucky to be here, lucky that you have all been so open. I'm not saying this very well," stammered Martin.

"I'm glad to hear that and I'm not surprised at all. I hope your film is able to capture who she was. She certainly taught me a lot. I am a different person for having known her, without a doubt. Honestly, I feel honored that you want to talk to me. What exactly do you want to know? What can I tell you about her?"

"Antonio—tell me whatever you want. Tell me what you think is important. Tell me what you think people most need to hear or understand about who she was and what she taught you."

Antonio started to laugh… "Whew… where do I start? There were a lot of things that she taught me. You know, it is funny I didn't really see it happening when we were together. It was after we broke up that I was able to look back and connect the dots and see how different I was from before I met her to after we broke up. But, I guess isn't that with most things… you don't get that clarity until you have had some time and distance from the experience. I remember one night."…

Sophia and Antonio were out on his boat. They had decided to spend a weekend leisurely making their way up the river and stopping in various towns for lunch or dinner. The sun was setting and they were relaxing after a full day and a delicious dinner at one of the restaurants along the river. Sophia had a glass of Cabernet Sauvignon in her hand. She sat reclined in her seat with her feet resting on one of her bags which had been lying on the floor in front of her. Her eyes were softly closed and there was a deep contented smile on her face.

She always looks so relaxed, thought Antonio. No matter what she is doing, no matter where she is, she is always at ease.

There was a place somewhere deep inside of him that craved what she had, to be able to feel that level of contentment. Even when he was relaxing, he was never really at peace. He just seemed to 'not be in motion' and that didn't necessarily feel very calm. There was always that damn feeling in his chest… that feeling that never seemed to go away, no matter what he did. He hated it, but he didn't know what to do about it. He was watching the slow rise and fall of her chest.

Sophia could feel him looking at her. She slowly opened her eyes and looked into his and smiled without saying a word.

"I wish I could feel what it is like in your body when I see that look on your face," said Antonio.

She started to giggle. "It feels delicious."

Antonio smiled back. "I bet." He got up and came over to her and leaned down and kissed her lightly on the lips, just a tease of a kiss, an invitation.

"Seriously, how do you do it? How is it that you always seem so relaxed?"

She looked at him softly, love and compassion poured out of her eyes. "It took a lot of work, Antonio. I didn't just wake up one day like this. First, I had to decide that it was a must for me, which it was. I couldn't live with that chaos and frenzy anymore."

Antonio nodded his head slightly.

"I know why you are asking, because I used to be where you are. It's an exhausting place to be, because you never fully let go. You're always running—from the past, from the pain, from the anxiety. I know that rhythm really well. I lived like that for a very long time until I decided I couldn't take it anymore. It was killing me, literally. You can do it, Antonio. It takes discipline and some courage, because it's not necessarily a pretty ride. It can get pretty ugly before you get to that beautiful place, but it is worth what you have to face and go through to get there. I swear. It really is worth it."...

"How do I start? What is the first thing?"...

"Well, there are a thousand ways to get there. You have to figure out what works for you. I would say the first thing is that you have to start getting quiet and pay attention to your body. Our body is always communicating with us, but most people don't understand the language of the body. Is there anything you notice about your body on a consistent basis?"

Antonio began without hesitation. "Yes, I have this constant thing in my chest. It's this kind of frenetic, squirrelly feeling in it... like a squirrel is racing in a circle over and over and over again. It makes it hard for me to breathe. I can only get a shallow breath. I can't stand it."

She rubbed her hand softly up and down his arm. "Then, that is where you begin, my love. Just start BEING with that squirrelly feeling. The next time you become aware of it, stop everything that you are doing and connect with the energy. Try and discover what that energy is trying to communicate to you."

"It's there right now."

"Okay, would you like me to help you to connect with it?"

"Yes."

"Okay, sit down and get comfortable and then tell me when you have quieted your mind. I just want you to focus on how your body feels. Focus on that and then start describing it to me."

Antonio closed his eyes, started shifting in his seat to find a comfortable position and then he took a few short breaths. Within a few moments, he began to speak.

"I feel this swirling energy in my chest. It's that squirrel… that is always the word that comes to mind when I feel this. It's like a squirrel running in a circle chasing his tail. And the faster he runs, the more frustrated he gets because he can't reach it, it's always just beyond his grasp."

"Okay, great. You are doing really well. I want to ask you a question and I don't want you to think about the answer. I want you simply to ask the question to yourself silently and let the answer float to the surface because I want your subconscious mind to answer it. And whatever it comes up with, just say it, don't filter it and don't dismiss it.

"Okay" he said…

"Antonio, what is just beyond your grasp? What are you chasing?"

Antonio began to rub his chest. A thick, hard knot formed in his throat as he tried to speak… "I don't know—I guess—to feel full, to feel full inside, to not feel like I'm missing something, like I am not complete or good enough right now with who I am."

Her heart ached for him. She could feel his pain, but she knew better than to try and console him. He needed to feel this. He needed to acknowledge the pain. He had to honor all those emotions he had ignored for so long.

"I don't think I have ever felt like I was good enough. I don't ever remember a time in my life where I felt like I was good enough for my parents or my teachers or my friends."

His eyes were still closed and a tear started to slowly work its way down his cheek. He could feel his throat constricting even further. She watched him with tender eyes as he allowed himself to let go.

"We all feel this way, sweetie. Everyone goes through it. It is some crazy part of human nature to doubt our worthiness. It's all crap. Of course you are worthy. And, somewhere deep inside of you, you know that. You just need to clear away all the clutter and forgive all those shitty moments in your life that re-affirmed for you that you were not good enough."

"Tell me, Antonio, what emotions are racing around in that squirrel inside your chest right now? Tell me exactly what emotions are stuck in this swirling anxious energy?"

He squeezed his eyes tighter, as if the squeezing were helping him to focus… "Anger—sadness—rage—frustration—sorrow"…

Sophia looked over at him and was filled with such love for him. "This is amazing that you are doing this, honey; it's so beautiful. I know it feels pretty shitty right now, but you will see, it will help."

Antonio rubbed his chest, massaging the pain, and then took a slow deep breath to try and handle all the feelings that were flooding through him.

Sophia sat silently next to him, pouring her love through her heart directly into his, supporting him fully while he worked through this wound. She did not want to stop his releasing in any way; she simply sat with him, with total presence to honor his journey.

After a short period of time he opened his eyes and looked over at her. "Oh, my God, wow—that was pretty intense. But that feeling is gone, there is no squirrel right now."

He looked over at her in amazement.

A soft smile spread across her face. "Wonderful. Just so you know, he will probably come back, but when he comes back, he will be coming back with a different wound. We heal in layers, Antonio. We are like onions; we peel back and heal one layer at a time. You need to have patience and compassion for yourself as you take this journey."

Antonio looked over at her and nodded his head. "Thank you, so much. I don't even remember a time I didn't have that feeling in my chest. This is incredible."

"It's called loving yourself. And it is pretty incredible. When we learn to love ourselves, everything in our life changes."

"I bet it does," said Antonio.

He looked over at Sophia and smiled. "Come here." He pulled her onto his lap and leaned his face into hers, kissing her softly on her eyelids and then the side of her eyes. He squeezed her tightly in his arms and they lay pressed together in each other's arms and luxuriated in the soft sacredness of what they just shared together.

"Cravings"

*I*t was dusk and it was chilly and windy as Leonardo sat in a reclining chair on his terrace drinking a glass of Veuve Cliquot Pink. He usually didn't drink Champagne, normally preferring his scotch. He had ordered a case shortly after Sophia's death. It reminded him of her. He found that lately he had started craving those things that reminded him of her. He lay in the chair. Every ounce of energy had gone from his body. He was completely spent. His head was resting against the back of the recliner and his eyes stared into the delicate Champagne flute, watching the bubbles rise to the surface. One by one he followed the bubbles as they floated to the surface. Like watching a fire, it was hypnotic. Soothing, even. The birds had quieted down and he could hear the fizzing bursts from his crystal glass. A slight breeze sent the graceful weeping willows dancing through the air.

The graceful lines of the trees swaying in the wind were hypnotic. He loved those trees. He always had, even as a boy. His mother had always loved them. Maybe that is why he loved them, they reminded him of his childhood.

He looked around the expansive yard with its meticulously sculpted gardens. He loved his home, but it had been so empty and lost so much of its appeal after Sophia moved out. It was never quite the same after she left. There was a loneliness that pervaded the house that had not been there before she moved in. Her presence had added so much to his home and to his life. She was like a ghost that haunted you.

He had tried to date other women, but all the relationships were short-lived. Nothing ever lasted. He couldn't help but compare them all to Sophia and, of course, no one lived up to her. He knew it wasn't healthy, but he didn't know how to let go and move on. Once you have had a relationship of a certain caliber, how can you accept anything less than that?

He shook his head… "Useless questions" he muttered. "She's gone and there will never be anyone exactly like her." His mind was flooding with thoughts.

"You'll find someone different. But you have to at least give them a chance, instead of just rejecting them before you even know them," he whispered to himself. He'd had these conversations with himself so many times… but love is not reasonable. It feels, what it feels, until it no longer feels it… and you have to ride it out. You have no other choice.

He took a sip of the Champagne and let it rest in his mouth for a moment. He was enjoying the sweet, bubbling feeling as it swirled around his mouth before he swallowed. He closed his eyes and replayed again one of his most cherished moments with Sophia… one of those moments that you never forget, that never stops nourishing you, never stops seducing you, never stops invading your mind…

Leonardo and Sophia had just come back from Chateau Lenoire after dinner. It was one of their favorite restaurants. It had been a wonderful evening. The food was incredible as usual, and Sophia looked stunning in a pale pink shift dress. Philippe, the chef, had come out and joined them for a glass of wine after their meal. After a short visit, Leonardo shook Philippe's hand and thanked him for the meal. He was ready to head home, as he was exhausted from work. He was so tired of being tired all the time. It had been an incredibly stressful work week. He had two business deals that both closed that week and it had been rife with challenges. He was ready to crash in bed and get a good night's sleep. They went straight home and, after a beautiful night, they were climbing into bed. Sophia had on a luxurious vintage pink French silk peignoir set that he had brought back from one of his trips to Paris. She climbed into the massive mahogany California king-size bed and started kissing his neck. She climbed on top of him and pulled out an ice blue chiffon scarf. It had tiny delicate red and white roses on it. She leaned down and placed the scarf over his eyes. He felt himself tense up. He grabbed the scarf and pulled it away.

"I don't want you to do that," he said tersely.

Sophia pulled herself upright and looked down into his eyes. "Don't you trust me, Leo?"...

"Of course I do, but I don't want you to do that. We can do other stuff, but I just don't want you to blindfold me."...

She was silent for a moment. "Okay," she said.

She looked down at Leo. "Leo—where do you let go? You are wound so tight with your work, so focused, so intense, all the time. Is there any place in your life where you completely let go? Is there anyone or anything or any place that makes you feel safe enough to just—jump, without a net, without a plan, without your move-by-move strategy all lined up? Just allowing yourself to enjoy the moment, wherever it leads. Would I ever lead you astray?"

She looked deeply into his eyes without saying a word. She rubbed the side of his cheek with her hand, ever so slightly.

"Would I ever do anything to you that would hurt you? Or disrespect you? I wanted to give you something tonight. I wanted to express to you what I feel."

She grew silent again and looked down at the scarf in her hands. She was twisting it back and forth between her two hands.

"It's hard to have to suppress who I am because you are afraid ... or... unwilling to step into the unknown. If we can't be who we are in a relationship with our lover, where in the world can we express the deepest part of ourselves?"

Leo could see her body start to sigh, a sorrow filled sigh expelled out of the pores of her being. She climbed off of Leo and headed into the bathroom.

"I'm going to take a shower."

Leo was voiceless. He couldn't think of a single thing to say. He wanted her to stay, but he didn't know what to say that would make her get back in bed. His mind was one big grey static blur of fear and frustration. He could hear Sophia shut the door to the bathroom.

He got up out of bed and walked to the bathroom door. He put his hand on the door handle to turn it, but then stopped. His body was exploding with anxiety. His heart was racing, his stomach felt sick and his brain was chirping away relentlessly...

What the hell is the matter with you? Why can't you let go? What are you so afraid of? His mind was racing. I fucking hate feeling out of control—what if… what if… what if… He punched the door.

He turned and walked over to the bed and grabbed his silk robe and slid it over his naked body, went downstairs and poured himself a scotch. He went into the living room and sat down on the couch. He looked over at one of his favorite paintings. It was a woman dancing. The colors exploded off the canvas. The strokes were raw, wild and bold. Every stroke of that painting screamed freedom. He loved that painting. He loved it for the energy it emitted, the energy he craved, but couldn't seem to relax enough to allow himself to experience. He'd get to a point and then he'd feel himself freeze up. The thought of losing control felt like death. He didn't know where it came from. He hated it, but he didn't know how to break through it.

He stared at that painting for a long time without saying a word. He could feel a surge of energy building in his solar plexus…. a quickening… a strengthening…and then he picked up his glass of scotch, swallowed the rest of it in a quick gulp and then threw the crystal glass straight at the painting. The glass shattered and went everywhere.

Leo stood up, walked upstairs, threw open the bathroom door and walked over to the shower, slipped off his robe and opened up the glass door. He stepped inside the shower and threw Sophia up against the wall of the shower. He took her arms and lifted them above her head and pinned her wrists to the wall. He leaned in and licked the inside palm of her hand and then lightly brushed his lips against her wrists, then walked his tongue down her arm and into the crevice of her shoulder. He paused there for a moment just before moving down to the top of her breast. He circled her breasts endlessly with his lips teasing and taunting her without touching her nipple. She was going to have to ask for it. Her hips jutted forward and started naturally rotating in a circular motion rubbing up against him. He continued to circle her nipple without putting it in his mouth.

She moaned. "Oh Leo, please."

He smiled in victory and then placed her nipple fully in his mouth, massaging the tip with his teeth and biting down ever so slightly.

The water was spraying down on them. Sophia loved her showers hot, almost scalding. Leo's back was red from the scorching water. He reached around with one arm, shut the water off, and grabbed Sophia by the hips, threw her around him and carried her back to the bedroom. He threw her on the bed and picked up the scarf off the floor. He tied it around his eyes and then said, "Whatever you want, my love."

A look of joy playfully came over her face. She got up and took Leo by the hand and gently guided him face down on the bed. She went over to the stereo, turned it on and hit play. Diana Krall's "Look of Love" came on. She walked over, turned off the light and climbed on top of Leonardo.

She leaned down, pulled back a clump of his hair and whispered into his ear. "I want to show you the depth of my love, Leo. I want you to feel my love through the depth of your pleasure."

"The Lesson"

*I*t was toward the end of their second interview together. Leonardo and Martin were sitting in Leonardo's living room. Leo had just finished telling him about the snorkeling adventure he and Sophia had had to an uninhabited island off the coast of Fiji. Martin looked over at the painting that was on top of the fireplace. It was of a woman dancing.

"Beautiful painting."

"Yeah… I love it. It was the first painting I ever bought. I still love it just as much today as the day I first saw it."

"Amazing how some things can resonate with you like that, isn't it?"

Leo nodded his head… "Yup."

Martin stood up and excused himself to head to the bathroom. He stopped half way down the hallway, where there were three oversize paintings of white orchids. They were three paintings with a flurry of white orchids going up the center of the canvas, but each had a different color backdrop… the far left was fuchsia, far right was lime green and the one in the center was a deep lavender. The detail within each of the individual orchids was masterful and the intensity of the colors exploding from underneath the pure white flowers was captivating. Martin couldn't seem to pull himself away from the paintings. The energy of them was intoxicating and inviting… looking at them made him feel—energized, ignited… he didn't know how to explain it. He finally turned away and hurried to the bathroom. Within a few moments he was back in the living room.

"Leo, I was looking at those orchids in the hall… those paintings are incredible."… Leo smiled…

"Yeah, I get that a lot. I knew the minute I saw them that I had to have them. They are kind of a special tribute, to a very special day. Sophia stopped by the office one day to bring me some flowers—white orchids."

He gestured his arm toward the hall. "She happened to stop by just before a very important meeting. I was giving a presentation that morning for an investment that the company was considering. It was an important presentation because no one in the company wanted to do the acquisition. I was the only one in favor of buying this small manufacturing company. It was a family-run business and had great margins, but it was in a sector we had never invested in before, so no one on the team wanted to take the risk. My gut instincts told me that this would be an incredible deal and I had developed a personal relationship with the owners. I know that isn't smart, but it just happened that way. They were good people, really good people."

"I knew their intentions for the business and I could see their commitment and work ethic, but my peers were blinded by the fear of never having invested in this sector before.

I had been gathering my data to build my presentation for weeks, but the night before the meeting I had an inspiration on a better way to present the materials that I thought would be more impactful. In any event, Sophia shows up that morning with these orchids and, let's just say, one thing led to another and I never got to finish my presentation. I literally had to walk into the meeting and winged it.

"Here is the really funny thing. At the end of the presentation, my boss comes up to me and says... "You know, Leo, you have been with us for over 10 years and you've done some extraordinary work for us. But, honestly, this was the most compelling presentation that you have ever made to us for an investment. I can't believe I'm going to say this, but I think we should move ahead with this. Great job, seriously—great job. I think this company is a smart investment and could just be the start of a new investment area for us, in general," and he slapped me on the back."

"I sat in the conference room for quite some time processing everything that had occurred that morning. Sophia was brilliant. I had no idea, until my boss said what he did, that Sophia's little flower visit was highly strategic. She had pretended to not remember that being an important day for me. She knew exactly what she was doing."

"She knew that if I had presented this plan like I had done all the rest, it wouldn't fly. She knew that by me having to present it extemporaneously, that my passion for the project would have to sell it. And that by not having my outline, I would have to be completely PRESENT during the presentation, that I would be able to just follow along the outline, that I would have to grasp what I felt was most important.... and... by being present... I was able to moment-by-moment read the faces of everyone in the room and address their concerns directly at that time and bring it out into the discussion. I wasn't just ramming my agenda down their throat. I was reeling them in one by one and converting their skepticism to belief.... I know that had I done my normal presentation, it never would have flown."

"She was a genius, Martin... a genius... She saw and understood things that most people didn't see. She was always steps ahead of everyone else and did it effortlessly. She was so in touch with life. I still don't know to this day how she was able to see and understand things the way she did. I wish I had been able to figure out her secret. I'd ask her about it, but she didn't know how to explain it. She had done so much work and growth in so many different areas of life that she was able to layer all that knowledge and wisdom into the quilt that was her life. It was incredible to watch, and even more exciting to be a part of."

Martin was staring back in fascination. He took a deep breath and blew it out slowly.... "Was it intuition, do you think?"

Leo looked back and raised his eyebrows. "Partly. But, it was more than that. There were always so many elements at work: emotional openness, intuition, compassion, human psychology and business acumen. She'd synthesize all the things she learned and then connect them all. She'd connect something she'd learned in Reiki training and find a parallel in one of my investment acquisitions, it was bizarre."

"It was like she was an engineer, in terms of seeing how all the little pieces had to come together in a specific scenario. Except her product wasn't a mechanical thing, it was the ebb and flow of people and circumstances. She could so easily see the cause and effect of one's subconscious mind and how it was influencing them. She had become so proficient at it, that she could do it in real time. It was pretty wild."

"Sounds like she would have made a good therapist."...

"She would have, except that she didn't believe in therapy. She felt that the only way to really make any progress was to become your own therapist, because no one can ever know what is really going on inside of you, or what is best for you. She pissed off a lot of therapists with that view, but that's what she truly believed. And, after knowing her as I did, and all the conversations that we had about this stuff, I have to say, I agree with her."

Martin got quiet and pulled his eyebrows together. "Hmmmm, well now that you say that, I will admit, I have a great relationship with my therapist and I've been going to her for about 5 years, but I haven't really resolved anything. I just go there and talk…. And maybe it's just that she was there to listen and not judge me."

Leo smiled and nodded his head and then said, "and what if the person you need to stop judging you, is yourself?"… Leo then picked up his glass and took a sip of his scotch.

"Cocktails"

artin was in his bedroom and the radio was turned up loud. Pink's "Raise Your Glass" was playing in the background. He was buzzing around his closet trying to figure out what he wanted to wear. His hips were swaying and his shoulders were rolling back and forth to the beat of the music as he perused his shirts...

I don't want to wear white tonight. I want something colorful, something fun. Something Sophia would have loved, he thought. His fingers rolled over the tops of several shirts and finally stopped at a periwinkle dress shirt. He smiled and then laughed... You're one lucky fella.

He slid it off the hanger and put it on. He shuffle-bopped over to his dressing table and dabbed a little cologne on his hands and then rubbed them together, smacked it on the side of his cheeks and down his neck.

He had invited Claudia, Gianna, Antonio, Leonardo, Tristan and Finnegan over for dinner. He had sent them all the manuscripts to "Sophia's Lovers" and wanted to gather them all together in one night to get their feedback. It felt like a half dozen dragonflies were flying in a swirling vortex in his stomach. He did a sleek catwalk into the bathroom to the sound of the music. He reached into the drawer to get his hairbrush and caught a glimpse of himself in the mirror.

He shot himself his best "Blue Steel" fashion model pose and put the microphone-hairbrush to his mouth "Don't get fancy. Just get dancy." He started dancing with himself in the mirror and belting out the lyrics at the top of his voice, thrusting his hips left and right...

"Why so serious? So raise your glass if you are wrong in all the right ways." He was singing so loud he barely heard the doorbell ring. He shot one last glance in the mirror and half-sang, half-screamed 'dirty little freaks,' threw the hairbrush at the mirror and skip-danced down the hall to get the door.

He was breathless as he pulled opened the massive Tuscan style door. Finn, Claudia and Gianna were standing there.

"Hi," he sang with a playful grin. They smiled back in surprise and gave a collective "Hello," as they started to laugh.

"Come on in. You guys are the first one's here." He welcomed them in and led them into his sunken living room.

"Your home is beautiful, Martin" said Gianna. He beamed with pride.

"Thank you. I designed it myself after a trip to San Casciano dei Bagni in Italy. I love Italy. I love every thing about it: the people, the food, the landscape. Everything about it feels like home to me." A smile of soft contentment washed over his face.

The doorbell rang again. He stood up. "I'll be right back," he said as he walked over to the door and opened it to find Leonardo. Martin smiled. "I'm so glad you were able to make it."

"It took quite a bit of finagling but I rearranged my schedule. I was supposed to be in London. I really wanted to be here for this."

He handed Martin an elegantly wrapped box.

"You didn't have to bring anything."

"I thought this was a pretty special night." He smiled. "And, I may be rude enough to ask you for a little," joked Leonardo.

Martin's eyebrows curved in curiosity. "You know I am terribly impatient. I'm going to have to rip it open right now," laughed Martin.

"I hope for my sake you do."

"Well, let me bring you in to see everyone and then I'll open it in there."

Just as they were about to turn to head into the living room, the doorbell rang again. Martin opened the door and there stood Antonio and walking up behind him was Tristan. Martin laughed… "Well, it looks like the gang is all here."

He shook both Antonio's and Tristan's hands as they came in and they all walked into the living room together.

Claudia looked up first, "Wow," she smiled... look who's here."

Everyone stood up and gave the usual handshakes and hugs. Claudia, Finn and Gianna sat back down on the long couch. Antonio and Tristan sat on another couch, while Leonardo took the leather chair angled across from the couches. Martin took the other leather seat next to Leonardo.

"I'm so excited that you all could get here tonight. I know a few of you had to move some important things and I really appreciate it. I'm very excited to hear your feedback and see what you have to say. But before we get started, I think I have to open this gift from Leonardo."

He laughed and then placed the gift in his lap as he undid the white bow and ripped off the shimmering, steel-grey wrapping paper. It was a 50-year-old decanter of Dalmore Scotch.

"There were only 60 bottles made," smiled Leonardo.

Martin was stunned. "Leo, oh my God. Are you sure you want to open this thing?"

Leonardo nodded his head. "Absolutely, I can't think of a better occasion to drink it and because obviously I want a glass."

"Will do," said Martin, as he got up and went to the bar. "Does anyone else want a glass besides Leonardo?"...

Finn, Antonio and Tristan all nodded and called out a very distinct and collective "yes"...

"I'm not really a scotch drinker. Do you happen to have any wine," said Claudia.

"Of course... Red or white?"

"I usually do white, but I love red, make it a red."

"And you, Gianna?"

"I'll take red too, that's fine."...

"Red, it is."

He took two crystal stem wine glasses out of the bar, poured two glasses of Cabernet Sauvignon for the woman and carried them over before opening the scotch.

"Sorry fella's, ladies first."

A generous chorus of "absolutely and of course" came back.

Martin walked back over and looked at Leonardo. "Will you help me do the honors?"

"Of course" Leonardo said. He got up and joined Martin at the bar. Martin handed Leonardo five crystal tumblers. "Can you get the ice while I open the bottle?"

"Sure thing."

Leonardo pulled the ice bucket over, grabbed the tongs and started filling the glasses with ice.

Martin looked at Leonardo as he opened the bottle. "Have to admit. I was pretty damn excited before you guys got here; this just puts everything over the top. This is awfully generous of you, Leonardo."

Leonardo looked over at Martin… "Call me Leo," he smiled. "I knew when I bought it, it was going to be for a very special occasion. I just didn't know which one. I won the bid in a charity auction so the money was donated to a local orphanage."

Martin smiled knowingly and shook his head. "Ahhhh, were you at that fundraiser with Sophia?"…

Leonardo started to laugh… "You had to ask."

Martin reached over and poured the deep golden liquid into the glass. The crackling of the ice was like music. He couldn't wait to taste it.

"Okay, Gentlemen, come and get it."

Antonio, Finn and Tristan all got up, came over to the bar and picked up their glasses. Then they all walked back to the couches and Claudia and Gianna stood up.

"A toast" said Martin… "This evening and this movie script are dedicated to Sophia, a beautiful, inspiring and loving woman who touched all of our lives and brought us together in friendship. May this film capture her light and true essence to share the message and purpose that was her life," said Martin, warmly.

A collective murmur of "Here! Here! and Amen" came from the small circle. They clinked their glasses and took a sip.

Martin spoke first… "Wow, that is one hell of a good scotch." He reached over and patted Leo on the back.

"Very smooth" said Finn.

"Absolutely, Finn. I agree, very smooth. Thank you, Leo," said Tristan.

Antonio was the last to speak. "Mighty fine glass of scotch, Leo, thank you." Within a few moments, everyone found their way back to their seats.

Martin took his seat anxiously. "Did everyone bring their manuscripts?" One by one they pulled out their manuscripts and put them on their laps. When every one looked up, Martin began. "Okay, let's get started."

"A Common Bond"

Gianna and Claudia were still inside the house talking with Martin. Antonio, Tristan, Finn and Leonardo were all walking out to their cars. The four of them stopped at Leonardo's car, which was closest in the driveway.

Leonardo spoke first. "This is kind of surreal, isn't it?"

Tristan laughed. "Yeah, that's for sure. Who would have thought?"

Antonio piped in next. "Guys, just think about who we are talking about. This is about Sophia. Of course it's surreal."

Leo shook his head slightly… "True." He paused for a second and then Antonio continued…

"If there is anything that I have realized from reading Martin's manuscript it's this: we were 4 lucky men—seriously lucky. She's gone and no other men on earth will ever get to experience what each of us shared with her." He paused for a moment and looked up at the sky before continuing.

"I don't know why I got to be one of the men that knew her in that way, that got to have a piece of her, a piece of her that will always be with me. I just feel so grateful. And you guys are the only ones who understand what I'm going through because you are going through it too.

"I've had other girlfriends since Sophia. But the relationship that I had with Sophia was different. It was—deeper… more than I've ever had with another woman. I know you know what I mean." Leonardo looked up first… "Yes, I know exactly what you mean."

Antonio was looking at Leo as he spoke. When Leonardo had finished, they all turned and looked at Tristan as he began to speak.

"The real question is—where do you go from here? Where do you go once you have had that? I think what we all got to share with Sophia was rare, really rare. What if it was one of those once in a lifetime things?" Tristan looked at each of them for a moment and then continued. "And, while I'm hurting that she's gone, could you imagine if we had never met her to begin with? Who would you be today if you guys hadn't been with her?"

The question lingered in the air as it seeped into their soul.

"I think Martin did an extraordinary job capturing her. And, after reading it, I feel closer to each one of you, because we all shared something very unique." They looked at Tristan and shook their heads in silent, sacred agreement. The silence was a moment of reverence, a momentary memorial to the woman who had brought these men together tonight.

Finn sighed a laugh and the other three looked over at him. "You know if Sophia was here, she would be laughing at us and saying that we hadn't learned a damn thing the entire time we were with her. That we'd missed the whole point, that sitting here lamenting her being gone and worrying about whether we would find that kind of love again in the future, that we were missing our life because all we ever have is this moment. Do I know if I'll ever have a relationship as amazing as what I had with her, again?—Who the hell knows. But, I'm here, now. I'm breathing and I'm open to whatever life is going to throw at me—the good, the bad and the ugly and I'm going to try to love it all."

"If we compare other women to her, we're going to suffer. And, I don't know about you, but I've done enough suffering in my life. I know the last thing that Sophia would want for any of us, would be to suffer. She'd want us all to be free, to have it all. I'm open to that happening again. And, that was her gift, her message, and her entire reason for being."

"I can feel her energy flooding through my body. I know that is the answer, wherever it leads."

Antonio stepped back and raised his eyebrows. "Wow, Finn, you nailed it. That is exactly what she would have said. You're right."

Leonardo was quiet. He looked at Finn as he pursed his lips closed and nodded his head the slightest bit. Tristan looked at Finn and shook his head.

There was a short pause and then Leonardo began… "I have to go, but I want you to know that I'm really grateful to have met you and heard your stories. It gave me even more to love about Sophia. I got to see other parts to her that I had not known through our relationship. So, thank you and let's stay in touch."

Antonio spoke first, "I feel the same way Leo, it's been a pleasure to get to know you, too."

Antonio reached over to shake Leo's hand. "Here! Here!" said Finn and he reached out his hand to shake Leo's hand.

Lastly, Tristan put out his hand and said, "Absolutely, Leo; I feel the same way. I'm not sure I'm up for catching the premiere of the movie together, I think that will be something I see at home; but I'd be up for a beer now and again," said Tristan laughingly.

"Beer it is," said Leonardo. "Night all." He bowed his head to everyone and got into his car.

Just then, Claudia and Gianna came out of the house and joined the group. She waved to Leo as he was pulling out.

"Oh, my God. What an amazing night. I'm still blown away by all this. Isn't it amazing that Martin just happened to see the article about her and that it sparked his interest? Kind of amazing how life works, isn't it? What a beautiful tribute to her life… and what a testament to his that he would pursue something like this when it was so far from what he had ever done before."

Tristan looked at Claudia. "Yeah, Claudia, I had been thinking the same thing recently. He never even knew her, and yet felt this connection to her from the paper. It's pretty wild. He did a beautiful job. He really captured who she was."

Claudia nodded her head in agreement. "Totally." She sighed… "What a great night. So is everyone ready to head home?"

Finn spoke first. "Yes, I'm wiped, ladies. I'm ready, if you are?"

Antonio walked over to Gianna and gave her a big squeeze. "So, you approve?"…

She smiled deeply. "Yes" she whispered, as tears welled up in her eyes.

Antonio smiled. "I think Sophia would approve, too!"

He turned and reached for Claudia. "Okay, give me a hug. I've got to head out. I've got a long drive."

She smiled and hugged him tightly. "So great to see you Antonio. Drive safe." She rubbed his back and squeezed him one last time.

"I've got to head home too," said Tristan, as he walked over and hugged Gianna and Claudia.

Claudia then announced, "I just want you to know how special you all are, to Sophia and to Mom and I. You will always be family to us."

"The Drive Home"

ristan climbed into his Saab, started the engine and hit the button for the convertible. When the top was down, he put it into reverse and pulled slowly out of the driveway. He clicked on the CD player. Ben Howard's "The Fear" came on. He was driving for about 10 minutes before his thoughts drifted back to Sophia.

He remembered their trip into NYC. He and Sophia had been meandering around the art galleries in Soho all day. It was 6 o'clock and they wanted to grab some dinner back in midtown near their hotel. They stood on the corner for about ten minutes until they were finally able to hail a cab. They climbed inside "Broadway and 45th please," said Tristan. The cab driver didn't respond. "Broadway and 45th," he said again.

"I heard you the first time," he barked back from the front seat.

Tristan looked irritated as he turned his head to look at Sophia. "Who needs that kind of attitude? What an asshole," he muttered under his breath.

The driver turned his head as Tristan said that. Sophia watched carefully. She squeezed Tristan's knee and then reached into her pocketbook and grabbed a package of Altoids. She opened it up and popped one in her mouth. She then extended her hand to Tristan and raised her eyebrows questioningly.

"Thanks," he smiled and grabbed one. Then she leaned forward and reached her hand over the seat to the driver. "Would you like one, sir?" The cab driver jerked his head around... he looked down at the Altoids... then he looked up in the rearview to see her face. She smiled back genuinely...

"Altoid?" she said.

The edges of his eyes softened. "Yes, thank you," he said quietly. He reached over and grabbed one.

"You are so very welcome," she smiled. "So, tell me, what is your name?" He paused for a moment in surprise and then responded.

"My name is Kelvin," he said gently.

"Nice to meet you, Kelvin. Thanks so much for taking us up to our hotel. We've been walking all day and we are pretty tired. We are just in for a little romantic weekend away," she giggled.

He looked back into the rear view mirror again. "Well, I hope you have a great time."

"We are, aren't we, honey?" She turned and looked at Tristan. He smiled back and squeezed her thigh in response.

"So how long have you been a cab driver, Kelvin?" Sophia continued.

"I have been doing this for about a year now; it's a second job. I have my own business. I repair and sell copiers for small businesses. Things have been a little tight, so I took this on to help cover the gap," said Kelvin. There was a tension in his voice.

"That's awesome that you have your own business, Kelvin. Good for you. There are a lot of people who dream of doing that, but are too afraid to take the risk."

Kelvin looked up into the rearview mirror again to look at her. His eyes scanned her face to see if it matched the gentle tone of her voice. Tristan was watching Kelvin, observing how closely Kelvin was paying attention to every word and movement Sophia made. He could see a slow transformation in the cab driver from the moment Sophia reached out to him with those Altoids. He watched the two of them closely as they talked the entire way back uptown.

By the time they pulled up to the hotel entrance, Kelvin and Sophia were laughing and giggling about something. He must have gotten lost in his thoughts because he didn't even know what they were laughing about.

Kelvin pulled the cab up to the curb in front of their hotel and then quickly jumped out of the cab and ran around to open it up for Sophia. When she stepped out, he leaned in and whispered something in her ear. A huge smile exploded across her face and she said, "Absolutely." He threw his arms around her and gave her a deep, strong hug. As he did, he whispered something in her ear. Tristan could see her squeeze her arms even tighter around Kelvin. When they finished the hug, both of them were in tears.

Tristan looked on in disbelief. When he stepped out of the car, Kelvin threw out his hand to shake Tristan's hand. "So nice to meet you both."

Tristan extended his hand "Nice to meet you too, Kelvin. How much do we owe you?" Kelvin smiled and squeezed Tristan's hand a bit tighter. "Have a great weekend." He dropped Tristan's hand and ran around to the driver's side, jumped in and slowly pulled the cab away from the curb. Tristan watched the cab pull down the street and then looked back at Sophia with confusion.

"What just happened?" Sophia started to laugh. "It's called compassion."

Tristan looked down the street as the cab got smaller and smaller as it made its way through the cars.

"What did he say to you, when he hugged you?"

"He thanked me for asking his name and for the Altoid, for caring about him as a human being. He said that no one ever treats him like a human being. He said that people simply bark orders at him or ignore him all day. Then he told me that the reason that he was short when you first got in the cab is because he is stressed out because his daughter is very sick. This second job is to cover her medical costs."

Tristan felt a pang of guilt for calling him an asshole. "Why didn't he charge us for the ride, if he is doing this to make money for his daughter?"

"It was his gift. I thought about trying to make him take the money, but I knew that he would feel slighted. He wanted to give us that ride. He wanted to give back to me, for what I gave to him. How could I insult him and not allow him to give me his gift?" Tristan looked back again to see if he could see the cab. It was gone. He looked back at Sophia. "You never cease to keep teaching me things. You have a beautiful heart, Sophia. You really do."

He pulled her into his arms and squeezed her tightly and then kissed her softly on her forehead and then her eyelids and then her lips.

The doorman standing behind them turned and headed into the lobby to give them a moment of privacy.

Sophia looked up at Tristan "So do you want to head right to dinner or go upstairs for a little appetizer?" She smiled mischievously.

"Oh, I think I need a little appetizer. I'm famished." He laughed and then leaned in and lowered his lips down to hers and started to nibble on the side of her mouth. "See, I'm starving," They turned and headed in to the lobby through the glass door.

"Paying it Forward"

The cafe was bustling with activity as he sipped his morning coffee. His finger circled the top of the mug pausing at a small chip along the rim. He looked down at the edges of the chip and wondered how it happened. He looked up and across the small space and saw a family eating their breakfast. A little boy about 3 in a pair of blue jeans and a baseball shirt was standing up in the booth and staring into the table behind them. His mother kept grabbing him and sitting him down again, but he kept getting back up. He was smiling at the woman in the booth who was smiling back at him and playing peek-a-boo. A warm feeling spread through his chest as he watched the exchange.

The waitress came over and placed his scrambled eggs, bacon and toast down in front of him and refilled his coffee. He looked at her nametag "Luanne"… He looked up at her and smiled, "Thank you, Luanne."

She turned and looked down at him a little surprised. "Why, thank you." She stroked his arm in appreciation.

The bacon was crisp, just the way he liked it. He made a little sandwich with the toast, eggs and bacon. This was his favorite breakfast. It reminded him of his childhood and the Sunday morning breakfasts he and his family would have after church. Several different families would get together every Sunday after mass. It was one of his favorite childhood memories. The kind of memory that stayed with you forever, that brings a sense of grounding to one's life, a safe, secure memory to go to.

When he finished his breakfast, he reached his hand down into his left pocket and pulled out the pink nylon bracelet. He stroked it with a soft, reverence that had come to be the norm whenever he touched it. He thought back to what the priest had said to him and it brought him some small solace. He closed the nylon bracelet into his fist, squeezed it tightly and then put it back into his pocket. He paid his bill and headed out of the diner.

It was only a short walk to the small church that was just down the street. It was a beautiful day. The sun was shining and there were people out and about walking and roller blading. Couples strolled by holding hands and kids went by on their bicycles. He made his way around to the back door as he had been doing for the last several weeks, which is where all the volunteers would enter.

Once he was inside, he was greeted with a warm smile from Darlene, the Director of the Food Bank. She was a tiny little thing and had to be at least 70. She had been the Director of this food bank for over 20 years. It was her calling. She was like a loving mother hen overseeing this kitchen. She ran this program with the precision of a military operation yet, peppered with love, compassion and warmth. She interviewed every single volunteer personally before she would let someone into her kitchen.

"Morning!!—Wonderful to see you again. Got lots of work for you this morning. I think we are going to have a big crowd today. They started lining up pretty early this morning," she said emphatically.

"Just put me to work," he said.

She sent him into the kitchen to help Max, the head cook… "Hey, Max," he smiled as he walked into the kitchen.

'Today you are on scrambled eggs duty. Can you take over for me here and just keep stirring these?" asked Max.

"Sure, I think I can handle that." He stirred the eggs and watched as the volunteers poured in to set up for breakfast. Everyone was buzzing around with a smile on their face and you could tell that everyone who was there was there because they loved to give, that it brought them great joy to care about others, to want to lift another human being up. He had never in his life been in an environment like this before. He had never seen so many compassionate people in one place. No one got paid. They came here on their own time and many donated food every week.

He felt such gratitude that life had led him to this experience. It was a gratitude that was tinged with pain, a pain he didn't know would ever leave him, no matter what he did.

Forgiveness was a beautiful concept, he thought. But, how does one forgive something so terrible? He felt tears welling in his eyes. He wiped them away with his shirtsleeve.

The eggs started to bubble and thicken. He stirred them until they were the perfect thickness and then started to transfer them into the large metal pan. He poured the next batch into the pan and started stirring again.

"Okay, folks, time to open the doors," said Max. People started filing in very calmly and orderly and got in line. He looked up from his eggs and saw them with the eyes of a newfound purity. He looked at them through the eyes of love. He didn't see dirty pants and over-grown hair. He didn't see 'homeless people'—he saw divinity. He saw the fear in their eyes and felt the weight of their pain. He saw them not as strangers, but as family, the family of the beautiful, vulnerable, human race.

He finished up the eggs and brought the tray over to the table to be served. Then he picked up a pile of napkins and headed over to the line. One by one he greeted them, taking a moment to pause and look them in the eyes and make a warm, soft connection. Then he would hand them their napkin and maybe rub their arm or pat them on the back. Each one would get something, some kind of touch. He had learned about the healing power of touch since coming here. He could feel their gratitude.

In the past few weeks he had thought back across the entire span of his life and realized that there was not a moment in his life that he had experienced the kind of human connection that he had since starting to volunteer in this food bank. He felt very lucky. He might easily have gone his entire life without ever having experienced this. And this was quite simply—nothing less than the divinity of unconditional love. It took him until he was 50 to finally come to understand what the meaning of unconditional love was.

He looked down the line and then saw a young mother with three little girls. She was holding the youngest in her arms, the little girl was probably two and the other girls were hugging her legs. The baby in her arms was playing with her hair and the two wrapped around her legs were giggling back and forth with each other. He leaned forward towards the little two-year-old,

"Well, hello there young lady." The little girl smiled up at him and started to laugh and buried her face in her mother's shoulder.

"How are you doing my dear?" he said as he looked at the young mother.

She let out a nervous laugh… "Holding it together as best I can, I guess."

He looked at her warmly… "Better days ahead. Know that, better days ahead; you're stronger than you think. I can tell. I'm psychic like that."

He reached into his pants pocket and discreetly pulled out his money clip. He folded up the entire pile of money and he handed it to the young woman… "Treat yourself and the girls to a movie tonight or something, have some laughs."

She started to object when he raised his finger to his mouth and said,"shhhh… none of that… it's a gift, please don't hurt my feelings. I want you to have it."

She looked at him softly and tears welled up in her eyes. She shook her head up and down and whispered, "thank you." He looked back at her and said, "No, my love. Thank you."

He rubbed her arm and stepped forward to greet the next person. When he got to the end of the line he started walking back to the kitchen to get his next set of instructions. He was whistling. A sense of joy filled his chest.

"Actions Speak Louder Than Words"

*A*ntonio was fixing himself some dinner, his hands deftly moving about the kitchen with speed and accuracy. He had gotten home late and was quite hungry but wanted to make sure that he caught the Oscars tonight. He laughed as he thought about it because he had never watched the Oscars before. This was certainly not his cup of tea, but how could he not watch, and see if "Sophia's Lovers" won the Oscar. He had to admit, he was excited.

After much hemming and hawing he had gone to see the movie. He had been curious to see how his character would be portrayed. And he was surprised to find that he really enjoyed it, even though it was odd seeing someone pretending to be him. That part was a little surreal.

He threw the purple potatoes into the warm skillet, seasoned them with sea salt and fresh cracked pepper and tossed them back and forth until they were brown. Then he went back to the counter and combined the finely cut pecans, salt and pepper. He brushed the salmon with a thin coat of oil and applied the pecan mixture to the outside of the salmon steak and browned it for a few minutes on each side.

He was rushing to finish so that he could get settled on the couch. When the salmon was brown, he put it on his plate with the potatoes and headed into the living room and set it down. He turned on the TV and clicked through the channels until he found the Oscars.

He walked back to the kitchen, grabbed a glass from his cabinet, pulled out a bottle of Cabernet Sauvignon from the wine refrigerator and poured himself a glass. He brought it over and set it down next to his plate on the coffee table.

He looked up to see that the awards had not yet started and quickly darted upstairs to get out of his dress clothes and throw on some flannel lounging pants and a T-shirt. He was back downstairs in a few moments and sat down on the couch to eat. Several bites into the salmon he started to think about Sophia…

It was a leisurely Sunday morning and he and Sophia were sleeping in after a great night of entertaining. They'd had three other couples over for a formal dinner party and it went on late into the evening. The conversation was interesting as always, but that was standard fair with Sophia's friends, there was always something new and interesting to talk about. There was no moss gathering on her friends' minds. They were constantly challenging each other with new ideas. He had found it a little overwhelming when he first started dating Sophia, but after a while, the curiousness and the out-of-the-box thinking had grown on him. His friends didn't talk about things like that, it was mostly just politics and sports, which is fine enough but once you have been exposed to such unique conversations about energy and matter, and heard some of the intense personal experiences of her friends, you couldn't help but find yourself drawn in.

Much of the evenings discussion had been centered around one of her friend's past life experiences and all the odd coincidences that had occurred in her present life that brought her to the realization that these were memories from a past life.

He had been a cynic about all of this stuff when he first met Sophia, but he had found after four years, he had become much more open to things than he once was. His certainty about things had waned and his comfort level with the unknown had intensified. He didn't realize it when it was happening; it was something that had crept up on him slowly, over time. He even surprised himself sometimes with the questions he would come up with in these discussions and the level of interest he genuinely had when they unfolded.

He had awoken first the next morning and was enjoying the quiet solitude of early morning. He rolled over and looked at Sophia sleeping next to him. He reached over and brushed the top of her hair ever so slightly. He loved to look at her when she slept. She looked so at peace, a wave of gratitude rolled through him as he looked at her. She shifted positions and then snuggled closely to his body. He could feel her arm as it shifted and landed on top of his shoulder, then the feel of her leg as she moved it up and over him. She lay half draped over him.

She opened her eyes slowly and a soft, dreamy smile spread across her face. "Good morning." She reached over and kissed him on the shoulder a few times.

"Morning," he whispered back. He pulled her on top of him and squeezed her tightly while he kissed her on the lips. "OMG, I have morning breath," she giggled.

"I don't care." He ran his fingers through her hair and pulled her head back, to expose her neck. He took his tongue and licked her from the base of her neck all the way up to her chin. Then he straightened her head and pulled it down to him and kissed her fully again on the lips and whispered, "I love you."

She looked into his eyes; her chest began to fill with warmth and tenderness. "I love you too, Antonio." She stretched out her long, lean body on top of his and rested her head on his chest. "I love listening to your heartbeat." She smiled as she said it.

"In fact, I love everything about you." She inched her head over and kissed the top of chest. "What do you want to do today?" she asked.

"I don't know. The only thing I have to do for work is book my flight and make my hotel arrangement for my meeting with the Hendridge Group. I want to make sure all my ducks are in line for that meeting. We have been going back and forth for two months trying to figure out a date when all their key management can be there and it's finally a go. Just setting the meeting feels like a miracle at this point. Now the next hurdle is convincing them to invest in the concept." His eyebrows furrowed as he spoke.

"I'm sure you'll convince them; you always get what you want. When is the meeting?" she asked.

"June 5th, I have to fly there though on the 3rd and I'll be having drinks that night with Erik Dodson, my contact. And then we are having a preliminary meeting with three members of his team on the 4th and then the 5th is when we present the entire concept to the Management Team."

Sophia was quiet. "Oh, I see."

Antonio could sense her entire body tightening, and then she abruptly got up. "I'm going to get in the shower."

He looked at her concerned… "Sophia, is everything ok?"

She didn't turn around; She kept walking toward the shower. "I'm fine, Antonio. Don't worry about me." She said it with a coolness that was unsettling.

He didn't know what it was, but his gut was telling him that the shit had just hit the fan. He didn't want to ask her though. He started spinning his brain to think about anything that he might have done, or forgotten. "What the hell could it be?" he mumbled and then said. "Oh, shit!"

He got out of bed and went down the hall to the home office that they shared and went to her desk planner. He turned the page of the planner to June and there in bold red marker it read "Paris" and the line stretched from June 1st—10^{th,} he looked over to the side of her desk and their sitting on top of the itinerary that she had designed, lay two plane tickets. He felt sick. He picked up the tickets and headed to the bedroom.

Sophia was coming out of the bathroom in her towel. He was standing in the doorway. She looked over at him and her eyes moved down to the airline tickets in his hand. He was watching her carefully. She looked up at him; her eyes were red and swollen.

He began, "Sophia, I…"

She cut him off. "STOP, there's nothing to say. I know how important this meeting is. It's done. And so are we. I'm going to pack my things. I'll have all of my clothes out of here by the end of the day and I'll call a service to have my furniture moved by the end of the week."

Antonio was looking at Sophia intently. "Sophia," he began again.

"Don't. There is nothing that you could say to me that would make me change my mind. I've had this trip planned for over a year. I've talked about it to you over and over. I don't even know how many times I've said to you how excited I am about going to Paris with you." She threw the towel on the floor in disgust and grabbed her clothes out of the closet and started to get dressed.

"Please, Sophia, let's talk about this."

She looked him directly in the eyes and held his gaze in silence. He could see the pain etched in her face. She shook her head the slightest bit back and forth.

"No," she whispered.

He could barely hear it, but he felt it. He felt a sharp pain in his chest. He stepped into the room and he took her by the shoulders.

"Sophia, please, listen to me. You can't move out, we have to talk about this."

She looked at him. "Actions speak louder than words, Antonio. What's that saying?—Your actions are screaming so loud right now, I wouldn't be able to hear you anyway."

She pulled his hands off her shoulders, walked into the bathroom and shut the door.

"Coming Together"

laudia and Gianna were busy in the kitchen finishing up the preparations for dinner. Claudia had made a pan of lasagna and Gianna made the salad and was cutting up the garlic bread when the doorbell rang. Claudia looked up, grabbed her glass of wine and took a sip as she headed toward the front door. The doorbell rang again and again in a buzzing fury. She was laughing as she opened the door to find Finn and Tristan standing on the front step with two bottles of Champagne and two huge grins on their faces.

Finn spoke first. "I'm feeling Oscar Pride tonight, I don't know about you!"

Claudia giggled. "Yes. Mom and I have a good feeling about this, too. Can you believe it? It is so exciting. Where is Leonardo?" she said.

Tristan responded, "He is running late. He said to start without him; he'll get here as soon as he can." They both stepped in and all three of them headed to the kitchen to join Gianna.

Finn walked straight to Gianna and gave her a big hug and a kiss and then handed her the first bottle of Champagne. Tristan followed suit and handed her the second bottle of champagne and gave her a tight squeeze and a kiss on the forehead.

"Well, I think we should save the Champagne until we know for sure. So how about a glass of wine in the mean time?" she said.

"Sounds good to me," said Finn.

Tristan nodded his head as he said, "Works for me."

Gianna poured the drinks while Claudia got their plates together and they all headed into the living room to settle in for the Oscar show.

"Oscar Pride"

$\mathcal{M}$artin had usually always loved these Oscar parties so much. Mixing, mingling and connecting with all the power players in Hollywood. The celebrities were out in spades on a night like tonight, however, none of that held any appeal to him tonight. He was in a very different place tonight.

For the first time, in a long time, he felt at peace. Regardless of what awards the film got, he was really proud of the film. And, the thing that mattered most was that it resonated with so many people around the world.

The film had grossed over $440 million. Audiences had connected with Sophia and her message. He had received thousands of letters from moviegoers who had been touched by the film. He had been invited to speak at groups around the world about the film and its message.

There was a place in his soul that felt intimately connected to Sophia tonight. It was a beautiful feeling and he wanted to cherish every moment of that feeling. To fully enjoy that connection, he found the thing that he longed for more than anything, was silence and solitude. He made his way through the crowd politely making his apologies and saying goodbye to all the most important players in the room.

"Never insult anyone in this town," he reminded himself softly. People's egos were quite sensitive here and even the slightest thing could make them feel insulted and it could impact you professionally for years. He'd learned that lesson very early on his career from a colleague who had paid dearly for one loose comment at a party. This was a fickle town and he was a cautious man. As he stepped further and further from outside the doors of the party he could hear the pulsing music of the party start to fade.

He paused for a moment on the sidewalk and lifted the gold statue up to examine it once more. Oscar: the Medal of Honor in the entertainment world."

He smiled. He had four others at home, but none of them mattered to him more than this one. He looked down at the inscription on the placard "Best Picture—Sophia's Lovers"…

He smiled and felt a weird mixture in his chest, at once both warm and soft and yet heavy and sad.

Thomas, a tall, thin young man with black hair, blue eyes and a fresh boyish face came over to him. With a huge grin on his face he practically yelled. "It is so amazing, sir. So amazing. You must be so incredibly proud." He gushed and then paused as he saw the look of quiet contemplation on Martin's face. "Oh, I'm sorry, are you ready to head home now, sir?"…

"Thomas, I think I'd like to walk for a bit. Just go back to the car and I'll give you a call when I'm ready to go. I just want to enjoy the night air and take a walk through the park for a bit."

"Good enough, sir. I'll be waiting. Congratulations, again, the Oscar is an incredible achievement."

Martin looked up at Thomas and smiled… "I have to admit, it is a good feeling. It is a good feeling indeed. A little overwhelming, but very, very nice. Would you put it in the car for me? It's beautiful, but a bit heavy for a walk."

"Absolutely, sir."

Thomas walked over, took the Oscar from Martin and headed off to the car.

Martin closed his eyes, took a long deep breath, exhaled and then opened his eyes and looked up at the stars.

Brilliant night, just brilliant. Everything is perfect. He started off towards the street to head into the park.

"*Karma*"

*N*ick stepped out of "The G-Spot", pulled out a pack of Viceroys from his shirt pocket and fumbled to get one out. Then reached into his jeans and pulled out his lighter. He squeezed the lighter a few times, it wouldn't ignite. "What the hell?" He turned it again and it finally ignited. He lit one up and headed to his car.

It'd been a long night and he had to be up for work in the morning. He struggled to pull his keys out of his jeans. The bulking mess of metal was stuck on something. He finally got them out and opened up the door to his grey Hyundai Elantra.

"Needs a damn paint job," he muttered to himself. But, she gets me where I need to go." He started to laugh, a deep, raspy cynical laugh. The laughter morphed into a mucus filled cough that whistled and wheezed.

He started up the car, pulled out of the spot without looking and then turned his attention to the radio. He was switching channels angrily, don't they have anything good on the radio anymore.

The streets were slick from a quick storm that had rolled in. Finally finding a station, he turned the volume way up and started singing along to Bon Jovi's "Living On a Prayer."

Nick got through about four lines before his head fell forward and he nodded off to sleep.

Martin was crossing the street heading for the park. For the first time in a long time he felt some small sense of peace in his soul. Maybe this is why the Universe had brought us together, for me to tell her story, so that her life could touch so many others. Maybe God had a bigger plan for the two of us than either of us could have ever imagined. He reached into his pocket and pulled out the familiar pink nylon bracelet and began rubbing it like he had so many times over the last few years. "I hope this is what you wanted, Sophia. I hope this is what you wanted me to do, for you."

He was deep in thought when he heard the blast of a car horn blaring incessantly. As he turned his head, he saw a rush of grey coming straight at him. His heart jumped and his eyes bulged as his body stiffened with fear just before impact.

Nick's car ran right over Martin and then slammed into a black Mercedes parked on the side of the road. Nick's body was slumped over the driver's seat. He was unconscious. Martin, gasping for breath, lay in the middle of the dark, wet street. He looked down at his hand and stared at the pink nylon bracelet and gasped for air.

The pain was unbearable. He was scared. He'd never taken the time to contemplate death before and now as it stared him imminently in the face, he was terrified. He was starting to hyperventilate.

Several guests coming out of the party saw the crash and ran over to try and help Martin. A man in a tux knelt down beside him and looked up and yelled "Andrea, call 911"...

She reached into her crystal-covered handbag and pulled out her cell phone. "Hello, I need an ambulance sent to the Fisk Pavilion. There has been an accident and a man is injured. He looks really, really, bad."

Martin's body started to convulse. He was losing a lot of blood. He tried to speak, but nothing would come out of his mouth. As his body was systematically shutting down he could feel his energy fading. His eyes were darting back and forth, he kept trying helplessly to speak but couldn't. And then, something extraordinary happened. A familiar feeling started to fill his body. He looked up and saw a white light coming down and engulfing his entire body as a deep feeling of peace flooded his being. He suddenly realized he was no longer afraid. All of the pain he had been feeling simply stopped. He felt nothing but a pure lightness of being—as if he was floating on warm, soft air.

The two couples huddled around Martin watched in awe. No one spoke as they watched this unfold before their eyes. They could feel the energy too. It was powerful, intense. As the light started to recede back into the sky, Martin could feel himself leaving his body. He could feel himself being lifted into the light. The man in the tuxedo was leaning over Martin and holding his hand when the last bit of life force exited Martin's body. He could feel the grip loosen and the light leaving Martin's eyes. He had never witnessed anyone dying before. He stared at Martin for some time after he had passed. He wanted to say something but he didn't know what to say. He didn't want to move. He felt frozen in this moment.

The sound of the ambulance brought him out of his daze. He unclasped his hand from Martin's. He saw the pink nylon bracelet in Martin's hand and took it. He didn't know why, he just wanted it. He put the pink nylon bracelet in his pants pocket, stood up and walked back to his wife. He took her in his arms and held her closely. Tears were in both of their eyes. They stood trembling with gratitude for the love they felt for each other and for the realization that life is so very precious.

Christine Regan Lake

Christine is a writer, healer and self-taught contemporary portrait and nude-figurative painter who was born in New York in 1969. Her unique journey, which has included a rich cross section of experiences, has helped define who she is, how she lives her life and the kind of legacy she wishes to leave behind.

"Writing and painting are spiritual experiences for me. It is the expression of my deepest essence. Whatever I am thinking or feeling in that moment shows up in my work. As an artist, I am drawn to both portraits and nude figurative paintings for their ability to tell stories about the human experience. I have always been fascinated by the journey of the soul... the exploration of both the light and the dark within our selves and how we each make our way through the world with those parts of ourselves. I am a storyteller. I like my writing and my paintings to take my readers and viewers on a journey... to have my work be a catalyst for inner-reflection."

Prior to embracing her passion for the arts, Christine was a marketing professional who founded Redlake Marketing, a full-service advertising agency. She earned her Bachelors Degree in Business Administration from Ramapo College of New Jersey and is a veteran of the United States Army Military

Intelligence Reserve Corps. During her six-year tenure, she earned combat medals for her service in Saudi Arabia in 1991 during Operation Desert Shield/Storm, as well as receiving Army Commendation and Achievement medals for her work with the Central Intelligence Agency and the Drug Enforcement Agency.

In 1995, she was selected to be a Goodwill Ambassador to India for the Rotary International, where she traveled to India for 5 weeks and visited 15 cities while meeting with business leaders, government agencies, industrial organizations and educational institutions in an effort to foster understanding and improved business relations. Christine is a passionate world traveler who's adventures have taken her from snorkeling the coral reefs of uninhabited islands off the coast of Fiji and hiking into the Yanshan Mountain Ranges and then walking back down into civilization atop the Great Wall of China to trekking in the Himalayas with a Canadian trekking team to Base Camp on Mount Everest and aNational Geographic expedition to Antarctica.

Christine is also the founder of the Heartylicious, LLC which is addition to offering a gallery of her fine art work also has a division; Heartylicious Clothing www.HeartyliciousClothing.com which currently has a line of playful t-shirts that share uplifting and empowering messages for women and will continue to expand to other products that uplift and empower women. Christine chose to work with a vendor that was aligned with her values and could guarantee her that the shirts would not be made in sweatshops. And, a portion of all the proceeds from the t-shirt line are donated to the non-profit fund; The Lake Foundation to support and empower women, children and veterans in crisis.

Christine has long embraced her role as a Global Citizen and contributed both her time and money to causes that she is passionate about. She has received the Rising Star Award, President's Award from the Orange County Chamber of Commerce, The Spirit of Literacy Award and in November of 2002 Christine was selected to speak at the Wharton School of Business on the challenges of entrepreneurship at their fifth annual Entrepreneurship Conference. For over ten years she actively supported and engaged in the human rights efforts of Equality

Now an organization dedicated to ending violence and discrimination against girls and women around the world.

In 2009, Christine co-founded The Lake Foundation, which is a fund dedicated to educating, inspiring and empowering women, children and disabled veterans. A portion of the proceeds from all of her art is donated to the foundation. Christine's passion for life-long learning has blessed her with a unique journey that has sculpted her as a woman, mother, artist, writer, healer and activist. She lives in Cave Creek with her two son's Parker and Cooper.

To contact Christine you can email her at
Christine@Heartylicious.com
www.ChristineReganLake.com

Other Works by Christine Regan Lake

Circle of Healing for Women

"The Circle of Healing is a book that will take the reader on an inspirational journey through the four phases of healing in the Circle of Healing: Old Wounds explores the wounds that have burdened our heart and soul and that have kept us from fully experiencing our authentic lives. The Awakening explores the thoughts, feelings and emotions that arise when one begins to notice that something within them is 'Awakening' and wants to come alive. Healing Thoughts and Actions explore the thoughts and actions that will further help one along their healing journey once they have been 'awakened.' Onward and Upward explores how to go beyond your own pain and use your unique journey to serve others.

"On this journey called our life, we travel along a path that is mixed with pain, fear, anger, exaltation and every emotion in between. It is these emotions that create the quilt that is the fabric of our life. These moments, each and every one of them indelibly leaves a mark upon our spirit. Those marks can be badges of honor or shameful scars that we keep hidden from the world. It is our choice to decide which one it will be; honor or shame. Everything in this world is the meaning we place upon it. It is our choice to view the circumstances of our life from a positive or negative lens. We decide each and every moment.

The depth and intensity of the joy and fulfillment in our life is in direct proportion to our ability to acknowledge, experience and release those old wounds so that we may continue along our journey and move up the staircase leaving behind old thoughts, feelings and beliefs that no longer serve us as we take our life to another level of awareness and being. Grace is living in the moment.

When we hold onto those wounds and hold tight to our stories—the stories that keep us in our victim mentality we remain powerless and our lives are left to the whims of our family, friends, employees and acquaintances. BUT, when we release those stories, those excuses and we fully own every thought, feeling and action that we chose to have, then we have reached a milestone. Now, we are ready to step out of the passenger's seat and into the driver's seat and set a course for a beautiful destiny that we design.

To those of you who are reading this and who will actively chose to hear these messages and take action to heal yourself from the wounds that have haunted you, I say Namaste. I honor your courage and wish you a healing and self empowering journey."

To purchase "Circle of Healing for Women" go to
www.ChristineReganLake.com

My Body Cleanse

An easily understood description of toxicity in the human body and the process through which anyone's body can be cleansed at the cellular level by following the simple process outlined throughout this book. The result of cleansing the body is greater energy, feeling better emotionally, and a stronger body capable of healing itself and keeping healthy long-term.

"Detox, or to give it its full name 'detoxification', has been around since humans first became civilized and is a very natural way of getting rid of harmful pollutants that may have built up in our bodies. This is critically important because those toxins and impurities are stored deep within the body's cells and slowly over time as you become more and more polluted, it begins to have a direct impact on your health. It saps your energy, weakens your cells, and, as a result, your body begins to fight back. One negative result of this pollution is that your body...your cells, which are trying to survive, begin to mutate. Those toxins in your body are a direct hazard to your body's health.

As a protective measure, your body takes action against those toxins to make sure they don't get near your vital organs and cause irreparable harm. It takes those toxins and wraps them in a little sack that is filled with water and then tucks them away in the fatty areas of your body, safely away from your vital organs. Why do they do that? The body does that because most toxins are acidic, and acid will literally eat through your vital organs and even your bones. Go back to your chemistry days in school....acid is a very powerful substance that can burn through many substances. To look at the power of acid, just look at your teeth. It is not sugar that rots teeth; it is the acid that sugar turns into once it metabolizes. The acid is what is rotting the teeth, or boring holes in them, so that people need to get cavities filled and/or have a root canal. If that is what acid can do to the enamel of your teeth, what do you think it could do to the soft tissue in your heart, or your lungs, or your stomach?

When you understand the incredibly negative impact that toxins have on your body, you will understand that these toxins will eventually, over time, make you sick, weak, overweight, and lethargic. If you want vibrant health, you must detox and cleanse your body of those harmful impurities on an ongoing basis.

Far too many people are scared of 'detoxing' because they don't understand how it works and what incredible health benefits are gained from it. They also erroneously believe that it will mean going without food for the entire process and existing only on water with the occasional shot of lemon juice. This is definitely not the case. Detoxing is a simple, yet and one of the most powerful ways you can build a strong foundation for health. It is a way of cleaning out your body, helping to give the internal organs a little breathing space, so that they can recharge and continue to operate as they should.

In this book you will learn just how to detox safely, with minimum discomfort, so that your body becomes clean, pure, and is returned as near as possible to its optimum state of well-being. When your body is maintained properly, you are setting the stage for long-term health and well-being."

To purchase "My Body Cleanse" go to
www.ChristineReganLake.com

An excerpt from Christine's next book....

"Bella's Blossoming"...

It was a dark, cold rainy day as Bella sat in the back seat of the car headed to the airport. She was exhausted. The weight and pressure of the last 7 years had taken its toll. Her husband had dragged out their divorce for 7 years fighting her at every turn. She felt as though it had taken every ounce of her being to make it through. Steven had been so angry, so bitter, so cruel. She knew going into it that it would be difficult, however, she never could have conceived how vengeful he could be. There were times that she thought she might have a breakdown. Her only life-line through this nightmare was her meditation. Without that, she probably wouldn't have made it through the seven years. She probably would have caved and decided to stay. Steven kept trying to manipulate her to stay. Looking back she found it astonishing that she had found the strength and the courage to leave. It had been a long time coming. When the kids hit high school she was at her breaking point and finally asked Steven for a divorce. She had no idea he would react so strongly. She honestly didn't even think he still loved her. Maybe it wasn't about love and it was more about his bruised pride that she would want to leave him. She didn't want to think about that anymore. It was finally over. They had finalized all their paperwork yesterday. It had been a dark and painful day for her. Some small sliver of her felt a sigh of relief, but honestly the most overwhelming feeling was just being overwhelmed. She had been focusing on this day for years... it was the finish line and she always thought that once she'd made it across the finish line, somehow it would just be over. Like a light switch... a clean break. It wasn't that simple. Life seldom was. She rubbed her eyes and looked out at the cars on the road. She was hoping Newark Airport wasn't a nightmare, but the weather was so nasty there was bound to be flight delays. She didn't have the energy to be upset about it. She didn't have the energy for anything. She'd used up every last ounce of energy she had on her divorce and had been running below capacity for months. She needed this getaway. She needed to refuel. She needed some solitude. She'd found this spa while ambling her way through Orbitz one night when she couldn't sleep and decided to just book it on a whim. She had booked it months ago not knowing how perfect the timing would be. Ten Thousand Waves was a spa fashioned after the hot spring resorts in Japan. She had always had a fascination with all things Japanese so when she saw the beautiful photos she just booked it. She didn't even bother to read anything about it. Something inside her knew the minute she saw the photos that that is where she was meant to go. She had been so excited when she booked it. She didn't have that excitement now. She didn't have enough energy to be excited about anything. She had just enough energy to push herself to pack and call the car service. The driver had started chatting early on but her silent nods quickly quieted him. He could tell she didn't want to engage. She was happy. She simply didn't have any small talk in her right now. She closed her eyes and tried to rest as the car slowed in the backed up traffic.

She could hear the rain slamming down against the roof of the car. It was a nasty storm. Her lower back ached as she sat in the car. She arched forward and rounded her shoulders and pushed her lower back out trying to stretch it out and give it some relief. It didn't help. Her body ached all over. She had booked several different spa treatments during her stay. She couldn't wait to have them done. It felt like her body was literally crying for attention and release. She felt as though she had 7 years worth of stress crammed into every little nook and cranny in her body. "Seven years" she whispered. She never could have imagined it could have dragged on for 7 years, but it had. It was finally over. She needed to find a job. She didn't have the slightest clue who would hire her. She had been a stay at home mother their entire marriage. Taking care of the house and the kids and volunteering for the kids school had been her entire focus the past 30 years. What am I qualified to do? she wondered. She could feel her chest begin to tighten up again, as it usually did whenever she thought about her future. A girlfriend of hers was an administrator at a Hospice facility and had been telling her for years that she would hire her in an instant. She had told her that she thought her gentle nature would be invaluable to her clients. Bella had never seriously considered the offer. She was always so busy making sure the house ran smoothly. But, now Bella had to get a job. It was no longer a choice. Bella started to well up with tears as she thought about this. She suddenly started to feel hot. She undid the buttons of her coat and undid her belt and opened up her jacket. She took a tissue from her jacket pocket and dabbed her eyes. She looked out the window and saw a little girl with her face pressed up against the car window and making faces. Bella giggled and raised her hand and gave her a friendly wave. The young freckle-faced girl jerked her head back and flashed a big smile and then began to wave excitedly at Bella. Bella laughed out loud. She started thinking back to when her babies were that small. She closed her eyes and thought about her kids. They had been so angry with her when they first found out about the divorce. It was a gut-wrenching day. She thought that they would handle it better being older, but her lawyer told her that older kids actually handle it much worse than younger kids. She had tried to spend a significant amount of time with each of them individually trying to see where they were at and to try and help them to understand it had nothing to do with them. In the end, they would all feel the way they felt and she couldn't control it... she just had to honor where they were at with it all.

Finally, the car pulled up to departures. The rain had subsided for the moment and it was just a light drizzle. The driver got out and opened up the door for her and then proceeded to get her luggage out of the trunk. He handed her the receipt to be signed. She took it and quickly signed her name. "Thank you so much. I really appreciate it." She headed inside and found the check-in and got in line. She closed her eyes and took a deep breath. "I'm really going. I'm really doing this," she whispered to herself. She looked around at the various passengers in line ahead of her. Right in front of her was an elderly couple. The woman was perfectly groomed and coifed. She looked impeccable. She had on a brightly colored yellow pants suit and pretty pink, blue, green and orange flowered scarf around her neck and she had a pretty crystal pin in her hair. They stood there patiently waiting. Her husband reached over and took her hand in his. She looked over at him and smiled sweetly. It made Bella well up with tears. When she married Steven she had thought it had been for life. She had always assumed that they would grow old together. Ahead of them was a family of four. A mother, father and two young girls. One girl was plastered to her father's leg.

She must not have been more than 3. The older girl, probably about 6 was holding her mother's hand, twirling her hair and staring at the elder woman's scarf. Ahead of them was a middle-aged business man. He had a small carry-on and he was impeccably dressed in a dark blue business suit. She watched as he pretended to be looking at his iphone, but kept stealing glances at the woman in front of him. She was every woman's basic nightmare. She was one of those PERFECT 10's… she could have been peeled off the cover of one of those hideous woman's magazine's. She was tall, thin and tan. She was wearing a royal blue dress that went down to about her mid-thigh with a pair of black sling-back pumps. She had long brown hair that went down to her lower back. It had the perfect amount of light blonde highlights to make it look like she had just walked in off the beach. She turned around when she heard a loud bang come from behind us. Her face matched her body. Flawless. Beautiful green eyes, high cheek bones and large full lips. The neckline of her dress was feminine, but not trashy, revealing just enough cleavage to keep men wondering. Subtle, sexy. So she was beautiful and classy. That made Bella feel worse. Bella looked down at her own clothes. She looked at her loose fitting pants and her button up blouse and thin sweater. She pulled at her sweater and inched it down lower over her hips. She had a sick feeling rising in her stomach and she felt a tinge of anger at the woman. "She probably takes her perfect body for granted. She's never known what it is like to hate her body. To be self-conscious in her body every moment of her life." Bella whispered to herself.

Bella turned away in disgust. Disgust at herself, and anger for the media machine that had programmed her since as early as she could remember to hate her body. Thankfully the line started to move and she grabbed her suitcase and took several steps forward. She pulled her ticket out of her pocketbook and looked at the departure time 9:45 am… She looked at her watch "8:55" she muttered in distress. "I hope I don't miss my flight." She shoved her ticket in the side pocket of her bag. The announcer came over the loud speaker "Flight 467 to Phoenix now delayed." The knot in her stomach tightened. She let out a sigh. "I just want to get there," she closed her eyes. She could feel the anxiety building inside of her. She could feel the tears forming in her eyes. "I'm tired of crying" she thought. She forced herself to stop. "I'm taking a vacation from my tears for this week. I've cried enough. I'm ready to smile. I'm ready to find joy and to feel lighter," she thought out loud. She rolled her head around in a circle to the right and then to the left. The cracks were loud and jolting. She visualized the massage she had booked. She imagined the practitioners strong hands kneading her neck like dough and his thumbs digging into her tight muscles. She started to laugh as she realized that that was the closest thing she'd had to a sexual fantasy in a long time. Stress and sex don't exactly go hand in hand she thought. "How can you relax enough to want to have sex when your redlining with stress over every single area of your life?" she wondered. The line moved forward again and she grabbed her suitcase and moved down the line behind the adorable little couple. It was 9:15 when she finally reached checked in. She handed her ticket to the agent and quickly asked "Will I still be able to make my flight?" The tiny Indian woman looked up and a huge smile crossed her face. 'If you hurry, I believe you will make it. Here… let me get security to drive you down." She picked up the phone and within a few moments a gentlemen in one of those airplane golf-carts was next to the line. She looked at the woman and asked "I'm sorry what is your name?" She smiled back "Madira". "Thank you Madira… that was so sweet of you." "You're welcome. Now go so you can catch your flight." Bella smiled and nodded her head in agreement. She walked over and hopped into the cart and they were off. She got through security quickly and within a few moments was boarding the plane. When she finally sat down into her seat she let out a huge breath of relief. "Okay…. I made it. We're off… and from here on out… I'm open to everything just flowing… I'm releasing any energy that might slow me down or back things up. I'm releasing all obstacles." She giggled to herself as she finished saying her little prayer of intention. "Deepak would be so proud of me," she thought.

She had just finished giggling to herself when she saw that woman again coming down the aisle. With her perfect face and perfect body and perfect dress. Bella could feel herself getting agitated. As she made her way down the center aisle the only thing Bella could hear in her head was… "Don't let her sit next to me. Please God, don't let her sit next to me.".… Sure enough in the next moment the stunning model-like woman was stowing her bag overhead and took her seat right next to Bella. Bella grabbed one of the magazines out of the pocket of the seat in front of her and started flipping through it. The woman was fixing her seatbelt and putting her pocketbook under the seat in front of her. When nothing was intriguing Bella in the magazine she reached down into her pocketbook and pulled out "Synchrodestiny" by Deepak Chopra and started reading it. ~

www.ingramcontent.com/pod-product-compliance
Lightning Source LLC
Chambersburg PA
CBHW030517260626
47157CB00005B/1787